This book was purchased
with grant funds supported
by the Institute of Museum
and Library Services under the provisions of the
Library Services and Technology Act as adminis-
tered by the Missouri State Library, a division of
the Office of the Secretary of State.

FEB 1 5

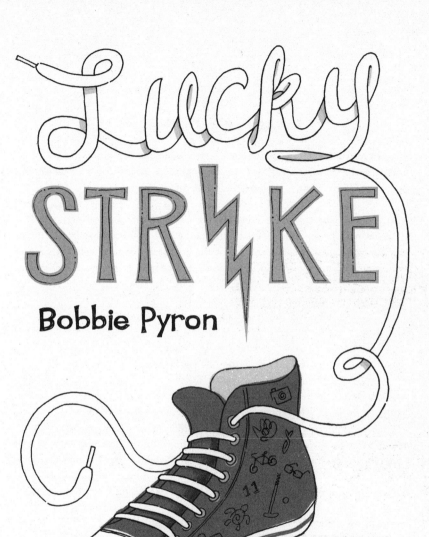

Lucky STRIKE

Bobbie Pyron

ARTHUR A. LEVINE BOOKS
AN IMPRINT OF SCHOLASTIC INC.

Library of Congress Cataloging-in-Publication Data

Pyron, Bobbie, author.
Lucky strike / Bobbie Pyron.
pages cm
Summary: Nathaniel Harlow lives with his grandfather in a trailer park in Franklin County, Florida, and he has always been unlucky — but when he is struck by lightning on his eleventh birthday and survives, it seems like his luck starts to change.
ISBN 978-0-545-59217-8 (hardcover : alk. paper) 1. Lightning — Juvenile fiction. 2. Life change events — Juvenile fiction. 3. Fortune — Juvenile fiction. 4. Grandparent and child — Juvenile fiction. 5. Franklin County (Fla.) — Juvenile fiction. [1. Lightning — Fiction. 2. Luck — Fiction. 3. Grandparent and child — Fiction. 4. Franklin County (Fla.) — Fiction.] I. Title.
PZ7.P999Lu 2015
813.6 — dc23
2014013764

10 9 8 7 6 5 4 3 2 1   15 16 17 18 19

Printed in the U.S.A.   23

First edition, March 2015

Book design by Ellen Duda

For Miss Bettis, who believed in me from the start

"Imagination is more important than knowledge. For knowledge is limited, whereas imagination embraces the entire world..."

– Albert Einstein

CHAPTER 1

Anyone in Paradise Beach would tell you that if one of their 313 residents was going to be struck by lightning — struck out of the clear blue sky on his birthday — that person would be Nathaniel Harlow.

Because wasn't it Nate whose hound dog was snatched up by a tornado, doghouse and all, never to be seen again? And wasn't it Nate who never, ever, in the history of his eleven years on God's green earth, won a coin toss or found a prize in the bottom of his Cracker Jack box?

Bad luck seemed to dog Nate Harlow's heels like his long-lost hound. Scrawnier than most, hunch-shouldered against the bad luck that rained down upon him, that boy was pure unlucky.

Nate awoke that spring morning of his eleventh birthday with an unaccountably light and fluttery feeling in his chest. He lay beneath his covers and listened. He heard his grandpa snoring on the couch in the living room of their tiny trailer. He heard the mockingbird singing its heart out in the magnolia tree outside his bedroom window. He heard the hum of the refrigerator and the steady *thump thump thump* in his chest. He did not hear anything that might account for the tiny flicker of hope fluttering like a moth in his heart.

"But it *is* my eleventh birthday," Nate declared to the mockingbird. "It's the *eleventh* of April on my *eleventh* birthday. That must mean something."

Nate did three things every morning after listening to the mockingbird.

First, he slipped his lucky rabbit's foot from beneath his pillow. His grandpa had given it to him on his fifth birthday, not long after Nate came to live with him. The foot, which had once been blue as the sky and covered with fur, was now brown and nearly rubbed bald.

Next, he touched the photo of his mother and father on his nightstand and said, "Good morning. I still miss you."

When Nate was four, his parents, who'd never, ever drunk a drop of alcohol, were struck head-on by a drunk driver and killed. That was the first time Nathaniel Harlow would learn that life can change in a flash.

And lastly, Nate slipped the camera his grandpa had given him for his ninth birthday into his pocket.

Was the unluckiest boy in Paradise Beach a budding photographer, headed for fame and glory? Not exactly. Nate took pictures — lots of pictures — but of only one thing: single shoes mysteriously separated from their mates. One flip-flop in the middle of State Road 102, a work boot lying lonely and forlorn on the side of Highway 98, a tennis shoe — just one — washed up underneath Henderson Pier. He used to pick up these orphaned shoes and bring them home with the hope that, somehow, the lucky day would come when he would miraculously find the long-lost shoe, reuniting the pair. That is, until their little trailer was overflowing with shoes.

Nate pulled on his shorts and padded into the living room. His grandpa sighed and snorted in his sleep.

He started a pot of coffee on the stove for Grandpa and fixed toast and a glass of milk for himself. The light, fluttery feeling in his chest held firm even though the milk had soured and the toaster burnt his toast. Again.

After all, wasn't it good luck that his birthday — his *eleventh* birthday — fell on a Saturday for the first time ever? And wasn't it good luck that his grandpa didn't have any fishing trips booked on his deep-sea fishing boat, the *Sweet Jodie*, and had promised to take Nate and his best (and only) friend, Genesis Beam, to play Goofy Golf?

"Maybe my luck is changing," he'd told Gen the night before. "My birthday has practically never, *ever* been on a Saturday, *and* it's my eleventh birthday on the eleventh day of the month."

"It's just the Law of Probability," Gen had said as the first firefly of the evening winked on and off. Genesis Beam did not believe in good luck or bad luck; she believed in the Law of Probability and answered to the Higher Power of Logic.

"Yeah, but Grandpa doesn't have any fishing trips booked either," Nate had pointed out.

"*No one* has had a Saturday fishing trip booked in a month of Sundays, you know that."

It was true: A run of bad luck had left the charter boats and their crews high and dry.

"With an average of fifty-two Saturdays in a year and your being alive eleven years, that's 572 Saturdays. Your odds of having a birthday fall on a Saturday are guaranteed."

"But —"

"It's odds, Nathaniel, not luck, just like everything else. Here, I'll prove it," Gen had said. She flipped a quarter high in the air and slapped it on the back of her hand. And as she'd done a million times before, she'd said, "Call it."

Nate sighed. "Heads."

She had pulled back her hand. "Tails," she announced. She flipped the coin again. "Call it."

"Do I have to?" he had asked. Gen glared from behind her thick glasses. "Tails," he said.

"Okay, so it's heads. That doesn't mean anything."

Nate swatted a mosquito.

For the next hour, Gen tossed the coin and said, "Call it," and he had.

Nate was wrong every time. *Fifty-three* times.

And like always, she had said, "There must be something off about this coin. If you toss a coin one hundred times, the odds are you'll get somewhere around forty and sixty heads. If you toss a coin twice, the chance of getting heads both times equals one-half times one-half, which equals one-fourth. And the chance of getting heads three times in a row equals —"

"But I was wrong fifty-three times!"

"For all practical purposes, that's impossible," Gen said, digging another coin out of her pocket. "The Law of Probability dictates —"

He sighed. Sometimes it was hard having the smartest girl in all of Franklin County as your best friend.

But even Gen doubted herself on that cloudless day of Nathaniel Harlow's birthday.

"Run on down to Gen's place," Grandpa said after he finished his second cup of coffee. "I'll load up the cooler with sodas and such."

Nate banged out the screen door. "Oh, and tell Mrs. Beam I got a mess of fish for her," Grandpa called.

He trotted down the road of the Sweet Magnolia RV and Trailer Park, the thick, sweet scent of magnolia dogging his heels. The crushed oyster shells gleamed white in the morning sun and crunched under his red tennis shoes.

"Morning Nate," Miss Trundle called from the wooden steps of her trailer. She waved her arm; the flesh beneath her arm waved too.

The boy stopped to pet one of her fifty million cats. "Hi, Miss Trundle. Today is my birthday."

"I know." She beamed. "You're eleven now. Such a big boy! Why, it seems like only yesterday when you came here to live with your granddaddy after your parents passed, God rest their souls."

"Yes ma'am," Nate said. And before Miss Trundle had a chance to go on about what all *else* seemed just like yesterday, he sprinted on down the road.

At the end of the trailer park, Mr. Wood called from his porch, "Happy birthday, Nate!"

He skidded to a stop on the oyster shells. "Thank you, sir. How are you today?" Mr. Wood's ancient Chihuahuas, Toots and Monk, barked behind the screen door.

The old man rubbed his knee. "My trick knee's acting up. Must be a change in the weather coming on."

A salty, fishy breeze from the Gulf of Mexico tickled the wind chimes in Mr. Wood's tree. Mr. Wood had chimes made of just about everything: bottles, seashells, tin cups, old forks and spoons and knives — all hanging from pieces of driftwood.

Nate glanced up at the sky, blue and cloudless as could be. "I don't know about that, sir. It looks pretty clear to me."

Mr. Wood waved the boy away. "Well, you run on now and have a big time on your birthday."

And he did. He left the oyster shell path and cut through the piney woods until he hit the red clay road leading to The Church of the One True Redeemer and Everlasting Light. The double doors of the white wooden church stood open, the voices of children tumbling out. He took the steps up to the church doorway two at a time. "Hey Gen," he called into the mayhem.

"Nate!" Two identical little girls in identical sundresses squealed at the exact same time. They raced each other down the long aisle from the pulpit to the front doors. They flung their arms around him, their scrawny black arms plucking at his shirt and squeezing his hands. "Happy birthday, Nate!"

He looped an arm around each shoulder and grinned. "Thank you Ruth, thank you Rebecca." Nate may have been considered a bit on the puny side, but when he was with Ruth and Rebecca, he felt ten feet tall.

The girls grabbed his hands. "We've been waiting all the livelong day for you," Ruth said, bouncing on her toes.

"We made you a card, and Mama made something special too," Rebecca said.

The twins dragged him past the worn pews, behind the pulpit, and up the steep side stairs to the living quarters of the Beam family. The smell of vanilla and chocolate filled the stairwell.

"Nate's here, Mama," Ruth announced. "Can we eat the cupcakes now?"

"Please?" asked Rebecca.

Mrs. Beam smiled. "Happy birthday, Nate." Then she shot a look at the two six-year-old girls hopping foot to foot. "And no, you may *not* have cupcakes now." The twins' brown eyes filled with sorrow.

"It's Nate's birthday," Gen called from the couch. "He gets the first one."

Ruth handed the boy a huge construction paper card decorated with hearts and kittens by the artistically inclined twin. "I drew you a masterpiece for your birthday, Nate! Do you like it?" Ruth twirled and spun out of the room before he could answer.

Rebecca tugged on his hand. "I wrote you a poem for your birthday," she whispered shyly.

Nate opened the card and read:

> Roses are red, the sky is blue.
> We sure are lucky
> To have a friend like you!

Nate grinned. "Thank you, Rebecca. It's the best poem anyone has ever wrote for me."

"*Written*," Gen corrected as she came into the kitchen. She handed a bag to Nate. "Happy birthday."

Nate pulled from the bag a book titled *Secrets of Florida's Loggerhead Turtles*. He grinned and ran his hand over the cover. "This is great, Gen. We can study it together since the turtles will be coming soon."

"I've already read it three times and have it pretty much memorized," Gen said with a shrug. "But I'll help you with it."

Footsteps pounded up the stairwell. Two identical little boys, two years smaller than the twin girls, raced into the kitchen. Yes, Mrs. Beam had had *two* sets of twins in a row. Gen would tell you the odds of that happening were one in seventy thousand.

"Is it cupcake time yet?" asked Joshua.

"Leviticus, Joshua," Mrs. Beam said. "You wash those filthy little hands of yours before you think about eating anything."

"Aw, Mama," Leviticus groaned.

"You listen to your sweet mama, son," a voice as big as God's said. Reverend Beam filled the kitchen. He laid his big hand on Nate's shoulder. "Happy birthday, young man."

Nate looked way, way up into the face of the reverend Beam and smiled. "Thank you, sir." Next to his grandpa and

Genesis, Reverend Beam was pretty much his favorite person on earth.

"Haven't seen you and your grandpa in church lately," Reverend Beam said as he always did.

"No sir," Nate answered as always. "But Grandpa says we'll be coming soon as we can. The pompano are running now, and Grandpa's always busy." Which they both knew was wishful thinking.

The reverend laughed a laugh as rich as the chocolate on the cupcakes. "And next the mackerel will be running, and then it'll be red snapper season, and then . . ." And it was true. The fishermen on the Gulf of Mexico marked the seasons by the run of the fish.

Nate had, in fact, asked his grandfather one Sunday morning why they, unlike pretty much everybody else in Paradise Beach, rarely went to church. After all, there were churches of every stripe and even a brand-new synagogue in their little town. His grandpa had put the last bait bucket in the back of the old green pickup. He'd squinted up at the sun and said, "We do, boy. We worship with Mother Nature herself at The Church of the Holy Mackerel." Still, Nate was happy that when they did go, it was to The Church of the One True Redeemer and Everlasting Light.

Mrs. Beam placed a yellow candle in the exact middle of the biggest of the chocolate-frosted cupcakes. Carefully, she lit the candle. "Make a wish, Nate," she said.

He stared at the candle.

"Wish for a unicorn!" Ruthie said.

"Wish for a kitten." Rebecca smiled.

"A robot!" Levi cried.

"A bicycle!" Joshua hollered.

"Hush now," Mrs. Beam said. "It's Nate's wish."

Gen rolled her eyes. She didn't believe in birthday wishes, and Nate wasn't too sure he did either. He'd just about given up wishing on stars and he'd never once found a four-leaf clover. There was the lucky rabbit's foot, although Gen never failed to point out luck had not been on that rabbit's side. He figured good luck had only visited him once in a blue moon. Still, he decided as he took a deep breath, it couldn't hurt, could it?

He closed his eyes and rubbed his thumb on the little rabbit's foot. *Please, please let something lucky happen today.*

Everyone watched wide-eyed as Nate unleashed a long, strong breath. Carried on that breath was 1) the wish that he'd have good luck just once in his life and 2) the knowledge that not only had his birthday wishes never come true, but the candles' flames had *never* gone out, no matter how hard he blew.

But this time, on Nate Harlow's eleventh birthday on the eleventh of April, a wavy line of smoke replaced the dancing candle flame.

CHAPTER 2

Grandpa swung his truck into the Goofy Golf parking lot. Heat waves shimmered above the asphalt. Grandpa mopped his brow with a red bandanna and tucked his white ponytail under his hat.

"Whoowee, it's a scorcher already," he said. "Good thing we got that cooler full of ice and drinks." Nate wriggled out of the passenger door and squinted toward the giant green dinosaur poised and ready to eat any golfer who dared venture too close. Smoke puffed from the top of the lopsided volcano, and an alligator's mouth creaked open and snapped closed.

"Here's your golfing money," Grandpa said. "The cooler will be on the front seat. I'll be across the street at June's. Y'all come on over when you're done and I'll treat us all to cheeseburgers and ice cream."

Even Gen brightened at this announcement. June's Back Porch had the best cheeseburgers in all of Paradise Beach, and probably all of Franklin County too.

Nate and Gen lined up behind the other kids to get their clubs, scorecards, wooden pencils, and colored golf balls.

Ricky Sands, the most popular boy in fifth grade, pointed at Nate and laughed. "Look who's here with his girlfriend. It's Shorty MacFarty. No use giving him a scorecard; he's a loser." The two girls on either side of Ricky giggled.

Nate looked down at the hole in his red high-tops and hunched his shoulders up around his ears.

Gen stuck out her chin and glared at Ricky. "I'm *not* his girlfriend," she said. "And Nathaniel has just as good odds as anybody of winning."

Ricky shook his head. "Figures the preacher's weirdo daughter would stick up for a loser."

Nate cut a sideways look at Gen and smiled. "Weirdos and losers stick together," he said under his breath.

"Through thick and through thin, amen," she said, finishing their official motto.

"What color golf ball?" the man in the golf shack asked when Nate and Gen stepped up to the window.

"Do you have green?" Gen asked.

Nate groaned.

The man sighed. The long ash on the end of his cigarette slumped and fell to the desk. "You know we don't have green," he said. "I told you that last time. Red, yellow, black, and blue. That's what we got, that's what we've always had."

"I'll take red," Nate said.

Gen pulled at the masking tape holding her glasses together. "I don't like red."

"Then take yellow," he said, trying mightily to be patient.

"It's a disturbing kind of yellow," she said.

Nate took a deep breath and counted to ten. "Then take black, Gen."

"But —"

"Come on," someone called from the line forming behind them. "Get moving!"

"Gen, *please*," Nate pleaded. Why, oh why, couldn't she just this once act like a normal person?

Gen grabbed the black golf ball and stomped over to the first hole.

"The first hole's the easiest," Nate said as he placed his ball on the moth-eaten felt fairway. He knocked his ball down the runway, up the ramp, over the moat filled with slimy green water, down the other ramp, and into the wide-open jaws of a grinning gator. The ball dropped into the hole with a satisfying *clunk*.

"Yes!" He pumped his golf club up and down. "Looks like my luck has changed!" Nate held up his hand for a high five. Genesis Beam did not do high fives.

"Hmph." Gen scowled as she eyed the ramp and the moat. "No such thing as luck being all one way or the other." She swung her club. Her ball fell into the slimy, stinking water.

"That's *un*lucky," he said. "Now you've got to rescue your ball."

She refused. "No doubt that water is infested with malaria germs." Without a backward glance, Gen marched off to the next hole.

Nate sighed and fished her ball out of the moat. He caught up with her at the volcano, waiting behind Ricky.

Ricky Sands eyed the scubbly slope of the volcano leading to the crusty mouth of a cave. He winked at the gaggle of girls. He puffed out his skinny chest and whacked the ball. It climbed confidently up the slope and into the cave, where it dropped into the cup.

"Yes!" Ricky crowed. "A hole in one!" Flames shot from the hole at the top of the volcano.

Ricky stepped aside for Nate. "Now watch the loser at work." The girls giggled.

Nate felt his ears turn red. He hit the ball into the one and only miniature tree on the volcano's flank. The ball ricocheted off the tree and fell into the hole at the top of the volcano. The volcano coughed and belched smoke.

Gen wiped at a smear of ash on her overalls. "That's okay, Nathaniel. Next is the windmill, and I'm good at that one."

Ricky Sands and his entourage of girls were definitely *not* good at the windmill. He cursed and threw his golf club down on the ground. The man in the golf shack hollered at him to watch his mouth or he'd have to leave.

Gen stepped over to Ricky and tapped his arm. "There's

one revolution per twelve seconds and there're four blades on the face of the windmill. The time between blades three and four is point-five-eight seconds, so —"

"Shut *up!*" Ricky barked.

She stumbled backward, tripped over the fake tree gracing the volcano (which promptly burped clouds of smoke), and fell fanny-first into the slimy, stinky, malaria-infested moat.

Gen whimpered and flapped her hands as if trying to fly away from her predicament.

"What did I tell you?" Ricky said. "A weirdo."

"You didn't have to yell at her like that," Nate snapped. "She was just trying to help you."

Ricky rolled his eyes. "I need her help like I need a hole in my head." The girls laughed like it was the funniest thing they'd ever heard.

Nate threw down his golf club (which brought another warning holler from the man in the golf shack) and told Ricky to take a flying leap.

"Come on, Gen, calm down," he said, pulling her from the moat.

"I've got malaria all over me," she whimpered. "I'll be dead before *my* next birthday."

He did his best to wipe the green slime from Gen's overalls. "No you won't," he assured her. "I'm sure they put all kinds of insecticide and stuff in that water to keep the germs out."

Her eyes grew big. "*Insecticide? Did you say insecticide?* That's even worse! I'll end up with cancer or grow a third eye or . . ." She trailed off with a moan.

Nate sighed. Goofy Golf on his birthday was not going well. He looked up to the heavens, to that blue, blue sky, and asked, "Why me?"

And very far off in the distance, way out over the Gulf of Mexico, thunder rumbled.

"Okay, Gen, last one," Nate said as he gazed up into the great gaping mouth of the Tyrannosaurus rex, poised and ready to bite the head off of anyone — a luckless boy especially — who dared get a hole in one. Because as everyone in Paradise Beach knew, if you got a hole in one on the T. rex hole, you won a free game of golf. Something that, in the history of Nate's now eleven years on God's green earth, had never happened to him.

He dug deep down into his chest and found that tiny flicker of hope.

As he placed his golf ball on the tee and eyed the long ribbon of green between himself and the T. rex, something approximating a roar gurgled from the dinosaur's mouth. Its jaws creaked open and closed; its small arms jerked up and down.

Nate shuddered. He took a deep breath and gripped his golf club. "This is my last chance," he muttered to himself. "My last chance to get a hole in one and show everybody I'm not a loser."

It would take a miracle of the highest order, he knew, to get a hole in one. Still, wasn't Reverend Beam talking all the time about miracles? The face of Jesus in a tortilla? Lazarus rising from the dead? Jonah inside that whale?

He felt an unaccountable wind push at his back, urging him on.

"Oh please don't eat me, Mr. Dinosaur," Ricky called from the sidelines in a high, girly voice.

Nate took a deep breath. He looked up at the clear blue Florida sky and said to whoever watched over luckless boys,

"Please, just this once. Please." He squeezed his eyes shut. He swung his golf club high above his shoulder, the head of the club winking in the sun.

"You can do it," Gen said. "The odds are in your —"

Nate never heard what Gen said next.

At exactly the same time, the brightest flash of light and a crack as loud as the voice of God shook Nate's world. And then it was as if the hand of God grabbed Nate (none too gently) by the hand, twirled him up and around, and flung him at the feet of the King of Dinosaurs.

The last things he remembered seeing were the creaking jaws of the T. rex as they closed down upon him; the last thing he remembered thinking was that birthday wishes never, *ever* come true.

Then he felt a rising, pulling him up with a thousand strings fine as spider's silk. The strings pulled him up through his chest and stomach and arms and legs and, finally, free of his skin, with a soap-bubble *pop!*

He floated through the air, an air spangled with a thousand million lights. It was as if every lightning bug in the United States of America had converged around him. They tickled his arms and head and chest. They filled him with delight and peacefulness.

Music surrounded him and carried him aloft like the most beautiful angels all singing to him at once, or like the choir at The Church of the One True Redeemer and Everlasting Light.

"He doesn't have a pulse!" a voice cried from below.

Nate looked down upon the people swarming around a crumpled body.

"Someone run across the road and get his granddaddy!" another voice cried.

"Call nine-one-one!" Ricky Sands hollered to the man in the golf shack.

Nate could not for the life of him figure out what all the ruckus was about. He felt fine. Finer, as a matter of fact, than he'd ever felt before.

Someone pushed through the crowd and crouched down next to him. His heart swelled. *Gen, bless her heart.*

He saw her pinch his nose, then cover his mouth with hers.

"Ewww," one of the girls said. "She's kissing him!"

She locked her hands and arms and pumped his chest — *one, two, three, over and over* — then breathed into his mouth again.

"Don't leave me, Nathaniel Harlow," she commanded.

He heard the wail of a siren in the distance. He saw his grandpa run across the road. He felt Grandpa's heart hammering in his chest. Nate wanted so badly to tell him it was all okay.

His grandpa threw himself down next to him and called his name over and over. Nate marveled at the tears streaming down the old man's face. He had never, ever seen his grandpa cry, except when Nate's parents had died.

"Come on Nathaniel," Gen said as she pumped his chest. "Losers and weirdos stick together."

With each breath Gen blew into his mouth, and with each call of his name, he felt the strings holding him aloft break, one by one — *Ping! Ping! Ping!* — until he felt himself falling, falling, falling back into his broken body.

CHAPTER 3

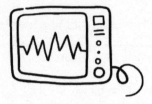

When Nate opened his eyes, he saw two things: his grandpa's worried, sea-weathered face hovering above his, and a complicated-looking machine beside him with flashing lights and zigzaggity lines.

Grandpa clutched his grandson's hand and said something Nate couldn't quite make out; his voice sounded like it was two miles away.

"What, Grandpa? I can't hear you." He licked his lips and tasted blood.

Grandpa leaned in close and shouted, "You're in the Panama City Hospital, boy. You were struck by lightning out on the Goofy Golf course."

Goofy Golf. The T. rex and his birthday. A loud crack and a blaze of light brighter than bright. A floating, hovery feeling. It all came back to him in flashes.

He licked his lips again. "Gen," he whispered. "Is Gen okay?" Every time he spoke, it felt like someone smacked a golf club against his skull.

Grandpa squeezed Nate's hand and nodded. "Gen's just fine. She saved your life with that CPR stuff she's always reading about."

Nate tried to nod his head. She was a walking medical encyclopedia, that was for sure. He had a vague recollection of her bending over him and pounding on his chest.

He wanted to ask his grandpa if he'd gotten to ride in an ambulance and if they'd run the siren and the flashing red light. That would've impressed Ricky Sands and all those giggly girls.

But Nate was so tired and cold, and his head hurt something fierce. So instead, he closed his eyes and held tight to his grandpa's rough, warm hand.

CHAPTER 4

The next time Nate opened his eyes, he saw the face of Reverend Beam. The reverend's eyes were closed and his lips moved, but Nate didn't hear anything except a loud rushing and crashing, like the Gulf of Mexico during a January storm.

"Did you say something?" he whispered.

The reverend's eyes flew open. "Praise the Lord! It's a miracle!" His voice boomed in the tiny room.

Grandpa's face appeared beside the reverend's.

"I told you, Jonah," Reverend Beam crowed. "The good Lord listens to our prayers."

Just then, the door to the hospital room swung open. A tall man in a white coat with a shiny stethoscope strode over to Nate's bed. A nurse bustled in behind him.

"How's our miracle boy doing today?" the doctor asked as he put the rubbery ends of the stethoscope into his ears. He parted the front of Nate's hospital gown and pressed the cold disc against the boy's chest.

Nate saw his grandpa's lips move. He caught a few words here and there: *deaf* and *gibberish* and *scars*. He looked with alarm from his grandpa to the doctor. The doctor poked a pointed black thing into his ear and took a good look around.

The doctor sat close to his left ear. "Nate, can you hear me?"

Nate frowned. Why did it sound like the doctor was whispering from the bottom of a wishing well? "I can't really hear you," Nate said.

The doctor wrote something down on his clipboard, then stuck his pen in his coat pocket. He moved so he could talk in Nate's good ear.

"It's not unusual for someone who's had a close encounter with lightning to lose some of their hearing, Nate," the doctor said. "Sometimes the hearing doesn't come back, but usually it does. Got a heck of a headache?"

Nate nodded, then wished he hadn't.

"That will hopefully go away in time too. We're going to change the dressing on your hand," the doctor said. For the

29

first time, Nate noticed the white bandage wrapping his right hand and arm like a mummy's.

"What . . . ?"

"That's the hand you were holding the golf club with when the lightning struck," the doctor explained in a voice loud enough for Nate to make out. "We figure it must have hit the head of your golf club, then traveled down the shaft into your hand. You were darned lucky, though," the doctor added. "You didn't take a direct hit. Most of the electrical force bounced off you and hit that T. rex."

"Blew half its head clean off," Grandpa said in wonderment.

The doctor began to unwind the gauze engulfing the boy's hand. "You're going to have some interesting scars, that's for sure, but at least you'll have a good story to tell."

They all watched as the unwinding of the gauze revealed Nate's hand.

"Yes," the doctor said, "it's a miracle you're alive, young man. A true miracle."

Reverend Beam grinned and slapped Grandpa on the back. "See, Jonah? What did I tell you?"

Nate gasped. Burned into the palm of his hand was a perfect imprint of the golf club's rubber grip, seams and all.

"Do you know what the odds are of a person surviving a lightning hit, even an indirect one?" the doctor asked.

Nate shook his head. Where was Gen when he needed her?

CHAPTER 5

A week later, Reverend Beam and The Church of the One True Redeemer and Everlasting Light held a fish fry for Nate and his grandpa. Like most of the fishermen in Paradise Beach, Nate's grandpa couldn't afford health insurance, and the fishing wasn't what it used to be. Nate had overheard his grandfather say to Miss Trundle that he might have to sell his charter boat to pay the hospital bills. When he heard this, he felt hot, then cold, then sick all over.

"My bad luck is catching, Gen," Nate had told her. "If Grandpa loses the *Sweet Jodie* and can't go out on the Gulf every day, I think he'll just shrivel up and die."

So Gen had told her daddy, and Reverend Beam had told the congregation of The Church of the One True Redeemer and Everlasting Light, who had voted straightaway on a benefit fish fry. Because, as everybody knows, there's not much a good fish fry won't fix.

Nate looked again at the grainy black-and-white photograph of the giant green T. rex at Goofy Golf, half its head blown to smithereens. The newspaper headline above it read MIRACLE BOY STRUCK BY LIGHTNING AND LIVES! If you looked real close, you could see something sprawled at the feet of the T. rex, something wearing just one red high-top tennis shoe. Where the other shoe went when the lightning struck was anybody's guess.

Gen thought Nate was awful lucky to have made the newspaper.

"When I won the Math Olympics last year, the paper only wrote two poorly punctuated sentences about it on the last page, next to the obituaries," Gen had said. "And did they run a picture of me and my trophy?"

Nate knew they had not. But they *had* run a picture of little Jimmy Revell, who'd won the junior division in the worm grunting contest over in Sopchoppy.

"Yeah, but the picture is mostly of the T. rex," Nate had

grumbled. "I just look like a bundle of rags at his feet. And they spelled my name wrong."

Gen tried not to laugh. "I bet no one noticed," she'd said. "I mean, *Nate* and *Kate* are almost identical," she snorted.

He'd sighed. "Yeah, right."

He wandered to the living room. He'd finally persuaded his grandfather to go back to his fishing boat. "I only have a half day trip today," his grandpa had said the night before. "I'll be back in plenty of time for the fish fry."

Nate plugged in the toaster and dropped in the sacrificial slice of bread. He waited for the smell of burning toast.

Instead, the toaster sang out the loveliest *ding!* you ever heard. Nate watched wide-eyed as a perfect, golden piece of toast popped up proudly.

"Must be a mistake," he muttered, and slipped in two more pieces of bread. Again, the toaster popped out the prettiest slices a person could ever want. "Cool."

Nate ate his perfect toast and listened to the mockingbird in the magnolia tree. Just as the doctor had said, the hearing in his left ear had, in fact, returned. He thought that bird had never sounded so sweet.

He got ready to go over to Gen's house. He pulled on shorts and carefully, very carefully, pulled a long-sleeve shirt over his bandaged hand and arm. Next week the bandages would come off. The thought of seeing what the lightning had left behind made the perfect toast flip in Nate's stomach. Would the scar of the golf club's handle be permanent? Would there be any other marks?

Nate stepped out the front door and studied the morning sky for even the slightest sign of a storm, then headed to Gen's.

"Where's everybody?" Nate asked the twin girls who were dressing up their cats, Shirley, Goodness, and Mercy ("Surely goodness and mercy shall follow me all the days of my life. . . ." Psalms 23:6). Rebecca held tight to Goodness while Ruth tied a tiny straw hat to the cat's head.

"Up in the kitchen cooking up a storm," Ruth said.

"For the fish fry," Rebecca whispered.

Nate found Mrs. Beam in the kitchen chopping cabbages for coleslaw. Gen shredded the carrots while Reverend Beam mixed his secret coleslaw dressing.

"Good morning, Nate," Mrs. Beam said with a smile. "You ready for your party tonight?"

"I guess," he said. He eyed the huge bowl of cabbage and carrots. "You're going to have lots left over, though," he said in a worried voice. "I don't think there's going to be that many people coming."

"Oh, I don't know about that," the reverend said. "From the talk around town, I think there's going to be more people coming tonight than you can imagine."

"Wow!" Levi called from his spot on the floor in front of the TV. "Maybe you and your grandpa will be millionaires!"

"I don't think the odds of becoming millionaires are very likely," Nate said. "Right, Gen?"

Gen shrugged. "Who knows? The odds of your getting struck by lightning are one in six hundred fourteen thousand seven hundred and fifty-nine, and you did."

"On a clear day," Joshua said.

"And your birthday," Levi added.

A shiver raced along the marks the lightning had set upon Nate.

CHAPTER 6

"Great granny's garters," Grandpa said when they drove to the corner of Billy Bowlegs Park.

They gaped through the cracked windshield as the ancient truck idled in the middle of Turpentine Street. Cars filled the weedy parking lot as far as the eye could see. Mr. Billy, the town's unofficial traffic director, waved cars this way and that with one hand while the other clutched his ever-present portable radio.

"There must be something else going on — a baseball or soccer game," Nate said, his eyes big as hubcaps. "Those can't all be here for my fish fry, can they, Grandpa?"

Grandpa threw the truck into gear. "One way to find out."

Grandpa steered the truck through the crowded parking lot. All kinds of people — some Nate recognized, some he didn't — strolled and skipped and raced to the park. Blankets and picnic baskets and small children hung from arms.

"Over here!" someone shouted. "Over here, Mr. Harlow!"

"That's Coach Hull from my school," Nate gasped.

Coach Hull trotted over to the truck. He grinned through the car window. "We've saved VIP parking right in front for the guest of honor. We don't want Nate walking all the way across the parking lot and getting struck by lightning again," he said, winking.

"Don't think that's too likely," Grandpa said. Nate made a mental note to ask Gen about those odds.

Grandpa pulled Alfred, the old green truck, into the parking space that was sure enough marked VIP PARKING.

He shut off the engine and patted Nate on the knee. "You look like you're about to be shot," he said. "It'll be fine. All these folks are here because of you."

"Yeah, but . . . but *why*?" Nate asked. "Most of these people don't know me well enough to say *boo* to."

Grandpa pushed open the truck door. "Spunk up, boy. It'll be fine."

Nate stepped out of the safety of the truck cab and eyed

the sky nervously. His grandfather took his bandaged hand in his own. "It's okay, Nate. I won't let anything hurt you."

Nate was about to say that even his grandfather couldn't control the heavens when he felt a warm surge of energy pass from his hand to his grandfather's.

Grandpa gave Nate's hand a careful squeeze. "Let's go enjoy the fish fry."

More people than he could ever remember seeing in his entire life covered the green grass of the park and the playing fields. Children raced back and forth playing tag and ambushing the unsuspecting with water pistols. Blankets and beach towels formed a giant patchwork quilt under the magnolias, live oaks, and palm trees.

And the most wonderful smells rode the salty air from the field house. "Mmmm," Nate said, closing his eyes and smiling. "Hush puppies." He could just taste one of those wondrous, golden, deep fat–fried balls of cornmeal, egg, chopped celery, and onion creating a symphony of joy in his mouth.

Suddenly, two squealing, bouncing things grabbed Nate's hands. "He's here! He's here!" Ruth and Rebecca nearly turned inside out with excitement.

Ruthie scaled his bony legs and clamped her arms around his neck, tight as a tick. "You're here, you're *finally* here!" She hollered so loud that, just for a moment, Nate purely wished his hearing hadn't come back.

Rebecca tugged on Grandpa's hand. "Mr. Harlow," she said, "you have to see all the food. Daddy says the folks of the church have outdone themselves *and* glory."

And indeed they had. Table after table groaned under the weight of shrimp casseroles, crab cakes, pots of gumbo, pyramids of sweet corn that would put the pharaohs to shame, buckets of coleslaw, baked beans, three-bean salad, potato salad, pans of fried okra, oyster pies, heaps and heaps of corn bread and biscuits, and, of course, mounds of perfect, golden hush puppies. Nate nearly swooned.

"Well, sound the trumpets of Jerusalem," a big voice boomed. Reverend Beam waved to Nate and his grandpa from a giant black vat. "Come on over and give me a hand, Jonah," he called to Grandpa.

Planks of fish and balls of hush puppy dough sizzled and swam in the fry grease. The reverend threw an arm around Nate's shoulders and spread the other arm wide. "Folks as far as the eye can see," he said. "*Hungry* folks, all more than willing to pay six dollars a plate to help you pay your hospital bills."

"I'd never have believed it," Grandpa said, shaking his head. "I didn't think there was this many people in all of Paradise Beach."

"Oh, there's lots more people here than just Paradise Beach folks," Rabbi Levine said as he lifted platters of fish and hush puppies. "I know for a fact some have come all the way from Port Saint Joe, Apalachicola, Eastpoint, and as far away as Wewahitchka."

Reverend Beam narrowed his eyes and nodded his head. "And they're all *hungry*, praise the Lord." He handed Grandpa an apron. "Don't think you're going to have to worry about selling your boat, Jonah," the reverend said in a low, confidential voice. "Now tie this apron on and help me round up the fish and puppies. We've got the multitudes to feed."

Grandpa wiped at a suspiciously wet eye.

"Nate, Gen's waiting for you over there in the shade. She's serving up the sweet tea and lemonade. I'm sure she'd like your company."

Sure enough, in the generous shade of the town's oldest live oak tree stood Gen, stiff as a log in a starched white dress. A pair of yellow rubber gloves reached all the way up to her elbows. She took the money from the thirsty like it was a long-dead fish. She handed the customers their drinks carefully so as not to touch them.

Nate stepped behind the table. "Hey," he said. "Thanks for doing this."

A small shudder ran through Gen. "It's bad enough I have to wear a dress when it's not Sunday." She took a particularly greasy dollar bill from a runny-nosed boy. "But I have to almost touch all these people."

"I'm sorry," Nate mumbled.

"I wouldn't do it for anybody else," Gen said.

"I know. Thanks," he said. "Really."

Gen wiped at a trickle of sweat on her forehead. Nate knew for a fact that Gen purely hated to sweat. Still, she smiled with one half of her mouth. "You know what they say."

"Weirdos and losers stick together," Nate said with a grin.

"Through thick and through thin, amen," they said together, laughing.

Just then, Ricky Sands and his little brother, Brandon, stepped up to buy their drinks. Nate busied himself pouring lemonade into cups.

"Can I see it?" little Brandon asked.

Nate looked from Brandon to Ricky. Ricky shrugged.

"See what?"

"Where you got hit by lightning."

Nate touched the bandages on his hand. "It's all wrapped up right now."

But little Brandon was not a boy to take no for an answer. "Well, shoot. Can I touch it then?"

Nate's face reddened beneath a plague of freckles.

"The kids all say it's a miracle," Brandon explained. "It must be like magic, right Ricky? Like superpowers?" The boy looked up at Nate with wide eyes. "Do you got superpowers now?"

Nate fiddled with a cup. "I wasn't really hit *directly* by the lightning."

"Yeah, but —"

"Cut it out, Brandon," Ricky said. "He was just lucky."

"Yeah, but —"

Ricky grabbed the back of the little boy's shirt. "Sorry,"

Ricky said to Nate as he dragged his brother away. Nate about dropped the cup of lemonade in his hand. Ricky Sands said *sorry* to him?

Gen laughed. "So now you're the miracle kid," she said. "Do you feel like a miracle, Nate?"

He shook his head. "I never in a million years thought Ricky would apologize to me. *That's* a true miracle."

As the dusky shadows stretched long across the grassy fields and as the seagulls fussed and fought at the overflowing garbage cans, Councilman Lamprey climbed up on the slapdash stage. A microphone squealed in his hands. He cleared his throat.

"I want to thank everyone for coming out tonight to help one of our own in need. And I want to especially thank all the good folks who aren't even from Paradise Beach for coming all this way."

Applause and whistles scattered the gulls.

"I always say we may not have the big fancy high-rises and resorts that some of the other beach towns have, but fishing folks look after each other."

"Amen to that," someone called out.

"Course, I wouldn't mind having some of that money all those tourists bring," Councilman Lamprey said with a wink.

"Before we start the football game, I'd like to invite our esteemed mayor to say a word or two." The councilman turned to a grizzled black Labrador retriever sitting at the bottom of the steps. "Mayor Barnacle Bill, would you please come up here?"

The dog trotted up the wooden steps, wagging his slightly bent tail. A red bandanna with the word MAYOR hung around his neck, along with an old dog collar.

"Would you care to speak a word or two?" Councilman Lamprey held the microphone down to the mayor's silver muzzle.

"Roof! Roo-roo-roof!" barked the mayor.

Everyone cheered. The mayor wagged his tail. Councilman Lamprey popped a hush puppy in the dog's mouth.

Coach Hull set about organizing a flag football game between a bunch of the kids from Nate's school and kids from their biggest rival, St. Mary's Catholic School.

After the teams had been picked, Reverend Beam stepped to the center of the field and held up his hands. Silence fell across the well-fed crowd. "I want to thank each and every one of you for coming out this fine evening to help our good friends and neighbors, Nate and Jonah Harlow." A wide plank of sunlight broke through the sunset and settled on the reverend's shoulders. "Now I know our little town hasn't had much to celebrate in a long while. What with the rerouting of the interstate and that hurricane year before last, we've seen some tough times. I reckon it's seemed like good luck has passed us by, like the tourists."

Heads nodded. Someone hollered, "You got that right."

"It's all them astronauts flying around up there," old man Marler called out.

In a lower voice, the reverend said, "But hard times bring out the best in folks. And here we all are."

Reverend Beam spread his arms wide, his big voice rising. "And then the miraculous happens: One of our very own gets struck by lightning — right out of the clear blue sky, I might add — and lives. *That*, my friends and neighbors, is something to celebrate!"

"Everyone seems to forget it wasn't a direct hit," Gen muttered.

The reverend smiled and turned to Nate and Gen, lounging on the sidelines. "I think it only fitting that Nate be the one to call the coin toss to see who gets the kickoff."

Nate suddenly felt cold all over. His head pounded.

The reverend continued, "And I'd like Nate's best friend, my lovely daughter Genesis Magnolia Beam, to toss the coin."

Gen shook her head frantically.

The reverend reached down for them. "Come on up, you two," he said. "Let's get this show on the road."

Despite the fact that Nate did not want to cause Ricky's team to lose, and the last thing Gen wanted was a million eyes watching her, when the good Reverend Beam reaches his mighty hands down and calls you forth, all you can do is go.

"Okay, boys," Coach Hull said. "Normally one of you'd pick heads or tails. But this time, Nate will pick." Coach sighed and shook his head. "Ricky, if by some miracle Nate actually wins the coin toss, our team will get to kick off. If not, well . . ." He patted Ricky's shoulder and said under his breath, "Sorry, son."

Coach turned to Nate and Gen. "Ready?"

The two friends stood in the middle of that field, the last of the sun's rays shining wide upon them. Nate looked nervously at the clouds gathering out over the Gulf.

Gen picked at her eyebrow. "Ready, Nate?"

Nate was purely not ready. He glanced across the field, his eyes searching and then finding his grandfather. His grandfather gave him a thumbs-up and a weak smile.

"You can do it, Nate!" Miss Trundle called.

He figured he might as well get this public humiliation over with. He touched the rabbit's foot in his pocket and nodded. "Flip it," he said.

Genesis Beam was probably the best coin flipper in all of Franklin County. The coin flipped end over end over end, higher and higher toward the sky. When it reached its highest point and hung there, suspended as if by wings, Nate took a deep breath.

Then the strangest feeling washed over him: a warm, glowing certainty like he'd never felt before. It was not frightening. It was true.

"Heads," he called out with all the confidence he had

never felt in his eleven years and one week on this earth. "It'll be heads!"

A hush fell over the crowd as Gen caught the coin and slapped it on the back of her hand.

Just like she had done a hundred million times before.

But this time, when Gen lifted the hand covering the coin, she gasped and her mouth fell open. Then it closed and opened again, like a stranded fish.

"What's wrong with that weirdo?" someone on the other team muttered.

"Gen," hissed Nate. "Make the call."

She held out her trembling hand for Coach and the good Reverend Beam and all the world to see. "Heads," she called out. "It's heads!"

Ricky Sands whooped. He and everyone else on the team grabbed Nate and hoisted him into the air like he'd just single-handedly won the football game.

A curious wind off the Gulf stirred the wind chimes in the tall pine next to Mr. Wood's trailer.

The wind carried the whoops and hollers from the crowd at the fish fry and the heave and sigh of the waves upon the shore. Toots and Monk, listening with their oversize Chihuahua ears, heard the splash of a pelican diving beneath the waves to catch its own supper.

And there. Just there. The faint thrum and beat of a hundred flippers stroking and surging their way — many miles away — through the green waters of the Gulf of Mexico. The flippers belonged to loggerhead turtles. Some turtles were returning to the white sand beaches of their birth for the first time to lay their eggs. These turtles were young at twenty years of age. Other turtles had returned many times before.

Young or ancient, it didn't matter. The moon and the currents and an agreement older than time pulled them to the sugared dunes of Paradise Beach, where they would pull themselves upon the shore, dig their nests, lay their eggs, and, by the light of the full moon, return to the sea.

CHAPTER 7

Monday morning found Nate fixing his own breakfast and telling himself to hurry up or he'd miss the bus.

"Sorry, boy," his grandpa had said the night before as he packed his cooler for the next day. "I got so many fishing trips lined up this week, I have to be out the door before sunup every blessed day." Grandpa bustled around the little trailer, smiling in a way Nate hadn't seen in a long time. "Don't know why my luck's changed, but I got to get while the getting is good! Got to ride this wave right into red snapper season," he said, pretending to ride the surfboard of his youth.

Nate popped two slices of bread into the toaster. He watched the appliance with an eagle eye while he stirred powdered cocoa into his milk. Yes, the toaster had been reliable lately, but he reckoned that wouldn't last.

Ding! Both pieces of toast sailed into the air and landed neatly, side by side, on the paper towel. The toast was truly wondrous in its perfection.

"Jeez Louise," Nate breathed. "Did you see that, Grandpa?" He turned to the couch, grinning. But of course, his grandpa had been gone for hours.

"I'm telling you, Gen," Nate said as the school bus bumped along the sandy road. "It was like that toaster had it all planned out. I wouldn't have been surprised if it had buttered itself and opened the jelly jar."

Gen looked up from her book on theoretical physics and sighed. "Nathaniel, a toaster cannot have a plan because a toaster does not have a *brain*." She shook her head and poked her nose back into the book. She'd just started the chapter on chaos theory and found it . . . well, disturbing.

"I know that. I'm just telling you what I saw is all. They landed right next to each other, neat as you please. What do you think the odds are of that?" He poked her in the ribs with his elbow.

Not looking up from her book, Gen said, "It's just like flipping a coin. If you do it enough times, the odds are in your favor. If the toast flies out of the toaster, as you claim, enough times, odds are they will land side by side one of those times."

Nate slumped in his seat and picked at the stuffing oozing from a tear in the vinyl. "It's not the same at all," he mumbled. "I *knew* that coin was going to land on heads. I felt it for a fact."

The bus pulled up to the entrance of Liza P. Woods Elementary. The familiar dread Nate always felt when he got to school lodged in his stomach like cold, leftover grits.

Gen gathered her books and pushed her glasses up on her nose. She watched the chaos of running, screaming, laughing, crying kids and sighed. She reached up to pluck at an eyebrow, then popped a rubber band on her wrist instead — Mrs. Beam's latest attempt to preserve Gen's eyebrows. Nate pulled the sleeve down on his bandaged hand and arm.

Gen blinked up at him. "Okay, it's your first day back. Are you ready?"

"I guess," he said, and followed his friend off the bus. He knew he'd feel a whole lot better about things if he could still wear his favorite pair of red tennis shoes, but at least he had his lucky rabbit's foot.

"See you back here after school," she said, like she always did, something that gave him comfort.

A spitball sailed through the air and landed in her hair. Nate plucked it out.

He watched as she walked down the long corridor, through the gauntlet of kids who laughed at and taunted her. Her backpack full of books hung almost to the backs of her knees. She was the only kid in school who had ironed creases in her jeans and the face of Albert Einstein on her backpack. For one single second, Nate wanted to run to catch up with her, to glare and holler at the kids who made her life at Liza P. Woods miserable.

It wasn't any use trying to protect Gen, though. They were the same kids who made his life miserable too. The difference, Gen always said, was he cared what those kids thought and she did not. *Easy for her to say,* he thought as he turned and headed to the other end of the building, where his classroom waited for him. She had the whole big, messy, noisy love of the Beam family behind her.

Nate pulled open the door to room 311. The cold lump of dread shimmied in his stomach. He hunched his shoulders, rubbed his thumb over his lucky rabbit's foot, and braced for the snickers and the eye rolling and the feet that would try to trip him up as he walked to his desk.

Instead, the tumult silenced.

Tiffany Hedges's and Chantell Peeks's eyes widened instead of rolling up into their heads. They studied him with wonder. Buddy Hayes poked Connor Marler and whispered, "Look, it's Sparky." Which Nate supposed was a better nickname than Loser or Shorty MacFarty.

He dropped his eyes to the floor, hurried over to his desk on the far side of the room, and slid into the seat. He wasn't exactly sure which was worse: the familiar taunting and tripping, or this silence and the way they looked at him like he was an alien. He was relieved when Chum Bailey — the only person in Nate's class who the kids teased more mercilessly than him — ambled into the room, his head newly shaved from his recent battle with head lice.

Chum had been christened Charles Rembert Bailey by his proud parents and Father Donovan at St. Mary's Catholic Church. The kids at Liza P. Woods Elementary christened him Chum because of his uncanny ability to attract those who preyed upon the weak.

Someone laughed and called out, "Look who's back! Chum the Bum!" Pencils, rubber bands, and wads of paper bombarded the big boy. The feeding frenzy began as Chum made his way over to his desk beside Nate. Nate scrunched down in his desk to avoid the fallout.

Chum dropped his book bag on the floor as a rubber band–launched paper clip whizzed past his ear. "Welcome back, Nate," he said. "I'm glad you're okay."

Nate scrunched farther down in his seat. Without looking at Chum, he said, "Thanks," out of the side of his mouth.

"I waved at you at the fish fry, but I guess you didn't see me," Chum said.

He had indeed seen Chum wave. "There were lots of people there," he explained.

"There sure were," Chum said, just as a shriveled, half-eaten apple bounced off the side of his head and landed in his lap. "You sure are lucky," Chum said, "being so popular and all."

Just as Nate started to explain that he hardly knew any of the people at the fish fry, Mr. Peck stalked into the room. His long, knobby legs, clad in tight black pants, ended two inches above a pair of white shoes. A dozen long strands of dark hair crested the top of his head. He reminded Nate of the great blue heron that hung out at the docks.

Mr. Peck glared at the mess strewn across the floor. He marched to his desk at the front of the room and banged his briefcase down hard. He put his hands on his hips and surveyed the classroom with a withering stare. Even the meanest, boldest kids straightened up and flew right.

"Good morning, my hooligans," the teacher said.

"Good morning, Mr. Peck," everyone mumbled.

"Good morning, teacher," Chum sang out, warm as a puppy. "I'm back."

"I see that," Mr. Peck said.

"The bugs are all gone from my hair now," Chum said proudly.

Tiffany snorted with laughter. Chantell made a retching sound.

Mr. Peck shot them a look sharp as a knife. "Thank you for that information, Charles." Then his pale eyes rested on Nate. "And welcome back to you, Mr. Harlow. I'm glad you escaped the slings and arrows of nature, as it were."

"Thank you," Nate said.

"You're most welcome," the teacher said. He removed his plaid jacket and rolled up his shirtsleeves. "Only thirty-seven days left of school, my rapscallions. Let's see what I can teach you before your brains turn to mush during summer vacation."

Nate could hardly wait to tell Gen about his day. Even though they were both in fifth grade, they rarely saw each other during the day, not even at lunch. Gen was in every gifted and accelerated class the school could think of. There had even been talk of advancing Gen two or maybe three grades, but her parents said no. "Brains don't necessarily equal good sense," Mrs. Beam had said. "Gen needs to take her time." Nate knew this was true; he also knew Gen had been sorely and deeply disappointed.

He waved from the back of the bus when Gen appeared at the front. Her shirttail hung half in, half out of her rumpled jeans. Her glasses hung crooked on her nose. Nate had a feeling she had not had a good day.

Gen plopped down on the seat beside him and hugged her backpack to her belly. She absently stroked the face of Albert Einstein over and over.

"You okay, Gen?"

Gen reached up and plucked at an eyebrow. "Fine."

"You don't look so fine," Nate pointed out.

She shrugged. "Just a difference of opinion with another student, that's all."

Nate frowned. She had twice been sent home from school this year because of these "differences of opinion."

Before he could bring this up, Gen said, "How about you? How was your first day back?"

"Oh, Gen," Nate said. "It was such a weird day."

"Weird how?"

"Nothing bad happened!"

He told her about how lucky he was that Mr. Peck hadn't called on him for the reading he hadn't done while he was home. "I kept thinking, *With my luck he'll call on me for everything,* but he didn't. Not once."

Gen shrugged. "Probably just felt sorry for you, wanted to give you time to catch up. Even though I *did* bring your schoolwork home for you, and even though I *did* offer to tutor you."

Nate ignored her. "And then at lunch, Mrs. Walker thought she'd given out the last Creamie, but then she just happened to find one that had fallen on the floor, so she gave me that one."

Gen rolled her eyes. "Yeah, that's lucky."

"Yeah, and just when I thought I'd have to sit with Chum Bailey in the cafeteria, Rico Sanchez and his cousin said I could sit at their table." He didn't mention they'd only wanted to see the burns on his hand. "And then in PE it rained, so we got to stay inside and watch a movie on oral hygiene," which to Nate's way of thinking was much better than not getting chosen for sides, or better than hearing Coach Hull say, "Good Lord, Harlow, you don't have the sense God gave a goose."

Nate leaned his head back and smiled. Yes, it had been a lucky day, indeed.

Gen rubbed at a smear of something red on her shirt-sleeve. "Yeah, well, add to your lucky list *not* being a preacher's kid." And then she pitched her voice low in a perfect imitation of the reverend. "Genesis Magnolia Beam, what kind of an example are you setting for your younger brothers and sisters, brawling and fighting? The good Lord and the rest of the world expect better from you." Gen took off her glasses and inspected the flap of tape holding them together. "I'll be writing out passages from the Bible from here to eternity."

⚡

Later that evening, just as Nate was thinking he'd walk down to the docks to look for his grandpa, he heard Alfred rattle up the oyster shell road.

"Sorry I'm late, boy," Grandpa called as he jumped from the truck. "You wouldn't believe the day I had." He caught

Nate up in a bear hug and mussed his mousy hair. "The fish, they just kept a-coming. My clients would reel one in, we'd rebait the hook, and then get a strike not two minutes after casting the line. I've never seen anything like it. Those two fellas — they were both from Knoxville — were so happy with their day, they gave me a fifty-dollar tip!" Grandpa reached into his fish gut–spattered coveralls, pulled out a fifty-dollar bill, and snapped it. *"Fifty dollars cash,* Nate. Can you believe it?"

"No sir," Nate said. "I hardly can't."

Grandpa ran his hand through his wild hair as if trying to tame his mind. "Good Lord, Nate, supper. Have you eaten supper?"

"I fried up a piece of baloney," he said. "And I was just about to open a can of tomato soup."

His grandpa clapped his hands together. "I'm so hungry, I could eat a whale. Let's go on over to June's and get those cheeseburgers I promised you for your birthday. Ice cream too. How does that sound?"

Nate thought it sounded like a perfect ending to a near-to-perfect day. "Can Gen come?"

"Sure can," Grandpa said. "Heck, we'll take the twins too." He stood in front of Nate and smiled. "But before all that, I have a surprise for you."

Nate frowned. He'd never been big on surprises. Life — at least his young life — had too often been scarred by the unexpected.

"Close your eyes," his grandpa instructed. "And don't look until I tell you to."

Nate closed his eyes and waited. He heard his grandpa walk away and then something clang against the truck.

"Okay, you can open your eyes."

He opened his eyes and gasped. There before him, the most beautiful bicycle in the world gleamed in the fading spring light.

Grandpa walked the bike over to Nate. "Happy birthday, son."

Nate ran his good hand admiringly over the gleaming handlebars and gear shifter. "It's amazing," he whispered. "It looks brand-new."

Grandpa nodded. "It is. I got it over at Peddle Pushers in Apalachicola."

Nate pulled his hand back. "But, Grandpa, we don't have the money for a brand-new bike."

"I've had it on layaway for months," he said. "I was going to give it to you on your birthday after we all had cheeseburgers at June's, but, well, then the lightning struck, and . . ." His voice trailed off.

Nate looked at the bike again. He took in the rubber grips on the handlebars, the reflectors on the spokes, and the leather seat just waiting for its rider.

Grandpa gave him a little push. "Why don't you ride it on over to the Beams' while I get cleaned up. I'll pick you up over there."

Nate fairly leapt onto the bike. If he didn't know better, he'd swear it was about to rear up like a spirited horse. He rode like the wind over to The Church of the One True Redeemer and Everlasting Light, skidding to a halt in front of Joshua and Levi with a flourish.

"Lookit that!" Joshua said, leaping to his feet.

Levi ran his little hand across the handlebars. "Where'd you get it, Nate?"

"Grandpa," he said. "He just gave it to me for my birthday." Now he wouldn't have to ride the old hand-me-down bike with the girl seat he'd been using for years.

"I can't believe I got a brand-new bike," he said.

"That means you got your birthday wish, right Nate?" Joshua asked.

He frowned. "What do you mean?"

"'Member, I told you to wish for a bicycle for your birthday."

Nate shook his head. In truth, he couldn't remember what all happened in the hours before the lightning strike. But wishing for a brand-new bike sounded like as good a wish as any, and if he had, well, that *could* mean his luck had changed, couldn't it?

CHAPTER 8

"Thank the good Lord it's Thursday," Gen said. She and Nate waited for the school bus beneath the tall pine crowned with a huge osprey nest — a nest so big, the littlest of the Beam twins could curl up in it for a nap.

"I don't think I can take another day trying to explain string theory to my science teacher." She zipped and unzipped, zipped and unzipped her backpack. "I bet it's been a long week for you too."

Nate shrugged. "It hasn't been as bad as I thought it would be." He'd gone the better part of a week without getting picked on, shoved around, or laughed at. Like a turtle barely inching its head from its shell, he almost looked forward to what the day would bring.

"Don't forget, we have to take flyers around town after school today reminding people about the Turtle Rules."

Every year, just before the loggerhead turtles arrived on the beaches to lay their eggs, Gen made it her mission to reeducate the good citizens of Paradise Beach about what not to do when the turtles came:

1) **NO OUTSIDE LIGHTS AFTER DARK!**

2) **REMOVE CHAIRS, UMBRELLAS, AND OTHER BEACH GEAR EVERY DAY!**

3) **FILL IN HOLES AND KNOCK DOWN SAND CASTLES!**

4) **NEVER, EVER DISTURB A TURTLE NEST!!!**

Each point was dramatically illustrated by the artistically inclined twin, Ruth. Rebecca sorely wanted to write the rules in rhyming verse, but Gen refused on the grounds it would make the rules less serious.

"According to my calculations, based on the previous years' tides and water temperatures and the phases of the moon, the turtles should be arriving within the next week or so." Gen felt the comfort of the steadfast turtles settle in her heart.

"Sure," Nate said. After all, did he have anything else to do with other friends after school? No, he did not.

Still, he wasn't thinking about nesting loggerheads and Turtle Rules. No, he was thinking about how lucky the week had been.

"Gen," he said. "I think getting struck by lightning changed something."

"Like what?"

"Me."

She cocked her head to one side. "Explain, please."

Nate fairly wiggled with relief to finally tell someone. "You and I both know I am just purely unlucky."

Gen pushed her glasses up on her nose. "Nathaniel, how many times have I told you: The universe is random. Things are not all one way or the other."

He held up his hand. "Just hear me out." He took a deep breath. "Ever since I got struck by lightning, lucky things have been happening to me."

"Like what?"

"Well, for starters, the coin toss."

"Odds," she said.

"And then all the things that've been happening at school — not getting called on when I don't know the answers, not having to sit at lunch with Chum Bailey, all those things I told you."

The bus pulled up. Before she could dismiss his evidence, Nate said, all in a rush, "And what about the toaster, and all the fishing trips Grandpa's had since I got struck, and my brand-new bicycle?"

Gen slung her Albert Einstein backpack on her shoulders and mounted the steps. "Random coincidences, pure and simple. And I happen to know your grandfather got you that bicycle *before* the lightning struck your golf club."

Nate followed Gen down the aisle of the bus. "I don't see what the difference is between luck and coincidence," he grumbled. The face of Einstein — eyes wide with surprise and wonder, hair looking like it'd had a close brush with lightning too — seemed to nod in agreement from Gen's back.

The kids snickered as they walked past; Gen frowned and said, "Nathaniel, you weren't struck directly by the lightning, which would have most likely killed you. Don't you think that's lucky enough?"

In PE that afternoon, Coach Hull blew his silver whistle. "We're going to finish out the school year with my favorite pastime."

"Eating?" someone asked from the back of the class. Snickers and laughter rippled through the room.

Coach's face burned red. He tried mightily to suck in his ample belly and tuck it behind his belt.

"No, smart aleck," he said. "Baseball."

Nate guessed it'd been a long time since Coach had actually been able to run the bases, but on the other hand, he himself had never been able to hit a ball. It was Coach Hull's theory that Nate and the bat and the ball did not speak the same language.

Outside, Coach divided the class into teams. Ricky Sands had groaned when Nate was assigned to his team, just like he always did. But it did seem to him that Ricky didn't protest quite as loudly as before. Still, Ricky gave Nate the oldest baseball mitt in the bunch and sent him to the far, far outfield — almost to the bay side of the peninsula. He wished just once, he'd get a turn in the infield, like everybody else.

Nate trotted to the far, far outfield and squinted in the sun as he watched the sky for clouds. Was that a rumble he heard off in the distance or was it his stomach? There were, in fact, clouds billowing out over the Gulf. He shivered.

And then he heard it: *crack!*

He dropped to the ground like he'd been shot and covered his head with his arms.

"Nate! Nate! Catch it!"

He uncovered his head and looked up. High against the blue sky, a white baseball arced lazily. The ball spun over and over, just hanging above his head, like it had all the time in the world.

"Catch it, Sparky!" Ricky Sands screamed from the pitcher's mound.

Nate didn't know whether to laugh or cry at the idea that he, Nate Harlow, could catch a fly ball.

But then, a tingling and buzzing burned his arm and hand; certainty filled him like a balloon.

He jumped to his feet and locked his eyes on that ball. He stretched his arm high and opened the palm of his mitt. And just like a homing pigeon returning to its long-lost roost, the ball dropped and settled pretty as you please in the cup of the leather mitt. Nate gasped and stared bug-eyed at that white ball.

He held the ball aloft, his arm still vibrating, for everyone to see. "I caught it," he whispered hoarsely. Then he yelled and yipped, "I caught it! I caught it!"

Mouths dropped open in disbelief. Gulls stopped their cries, and the wind stopped its humming. The silver whistle dropped from Coach Hull's mouth.

Ricky Sands leapt off the pitcher's mound and let out a whoop that could be heard all the way to the Florida-Alabama state line.

Coach stuffed the whistle back in his mouth and blew. "Out!" he cried. "Out!" Ricky struck out two more players in no time.

The teams switched sides. Mary Beth Malloy (otherwise known as Jinx) strutted to the pitcher's mound. She flipped her red braids over her shoulders and popped her gum.

Jinx Malloy was not only the best clarinet player in the school band, she had the meanest, snakiest knuckleball in all of Liza P. Woods Elementary. "We're sunk," Ricky Sands moaned.

First, she struck out Chum Bailey, which was not a hard thing to do.

Next, she struck out Ricky, which was near to impossible. His second swing went wild and sent the ball in an unfortunate direction, and his third missed the ball by a mile. "Out!" cried Coach Hull. Ricky threw his cap into the sand.

Next came Nate.

He crept up to the plate, gingerly holding the bat in his good hand. "Let's just hope the bell rings for the next class before she strikes him out," someone behind him said. And normally, he would have agreed: His chances of hitting the ball were about once in a blue moon, but hitting it one-handed with his *left* hand? It would take nothing short of a miracle.

But this time, something felt different. He paid no attention as Jinx Malloy grinned like a cat about to eat a wingless canary. He didn't listen as his teammates muttered, "It's all over now," and gathered up their books and packs.

No, he paid no mind to any of this. All he was aware of under that April sun was the conversation between the ball being smacked against Jinx's glove and the bat fairly dancing with anticipation in his good hand.

Nate unhunched his shoulders, stood up straight as an arrow, and grinned right back at Jinx. "Show me what you got," he called.

He didn't even remember swinging the bat. The next thing he knew, he heard a *crack!* loud as a Fourth of July firecracker. The ball sailed higher and higher in the sky, over Jinx Malloy's upturned face, over the first baseman and the outfielders. It hovered there for a second as if trying to make up its mind what to do.

"The ball got a second wind, I guess," he later told Gen. It gathered itself up and sailed on over the chain-link fence and out of sight. Later, folks claimed it was that same baseball that broke out the windshield of the brand-new 1992 red Ford pickup in the Crystal Sands New and Used Cars lot.

"Run, Sparky! Run!" Ricky Sands hollered.

Nate dropped the bat and sprinted from base to base, his grin getting bigger with every sandbag he passed. Jinx threw her hat *and* her glove to the ground. By the time he strutted home, everyone on his team was clapping and chanting, "Spark-*y*! Spark-*y*!" There were high fives all around. Nate puffed out his scrawny chest. Being lucky sure felt good.

"I'm telling you, Gen," he said as they walked to their bus after school. "It was like magic. It was like someone had cast a spell over that ball and bat."

She rolled her eyes. "There's no such thing as magic, and you know it."

"Yeah but —"

Gen ignored him. "It's not beyond the realm of possibility you could hit a home run."

He was just about to remind her he'd rarely hit a ball at all, much less a home run with one hand, when someone called his name.

"Hey, Sparky," Ricky Sands said, clapping him so hard on the shoulder, he stumbled. "A bunch of us are getting up a baseball game over at Billy Bowlegs Park. Want to come?"

Nate's mouth fell open. No one had ever invited him to do anything after school. No one except Gen, that is.

Nate looked from Ricky to Gen. "I, uh, I mean . . ."

Ricky gave Nate a shake. "Don't know what kind of magic possessed you out on the baseball field today, Sparky, but let's see if you've still got it."

Gen pushed her tilty glasses up on her nose and frowned. "Nathaniel and I have to pass out the Turtle Rules today," she said, not looking at Ricky or Nate, but at the space between them.

Ricky snorted. "Let's see. Your choices are to play baseball with us or go with *her*." He snorted again. "Tough choice, Sparks."

Gen frowned. "I beg to differ. Nathaniel is well aware of the gravity and importance of making sure the beaches are copacetic for the needs of the loggerhead turtles."

"Whoa." Ricky held up his hands to stop the onslaught of words. "I don't know what the heck you're yammering on about, Brainiac, but I'm talking baseball here."

Gen stepped closer to Nate. "Nathaniel appreciates how important the return and survival of the turtles is — much more so than some *game*." She looked at him. "They need us, right?"

Nate looked from Gen to Ricky, from Ricky to Gen.

"You're a *weirdo*," Ricky said. Pointing at Nate, he said, "And you're even more of a loser than I thought if you want to hang out with *her* and a bunch of turtles."

Ricky strode off through the crowd.

"Well, enough of that dunderhead," Gen said. "Let's divide up the flyers and —"

"Jeez Louise, Gen!" Nate exploded.

Gen took a step back.

"Why can't you *just once* act like a normal person?"

And before Gen could answer, he sprinted off. "Wait up, Ricky," he cried. "Wait for me!"

Gen's eyes swam behind her glasses. Her nose dripped. One hand worked at an eyebrow while the other hand stroked the face of Albert Einstein. Never, ever, in all the years she had known Nate Harlow, had he yelled at her.

She climbed the steps into the bus and took the very last seat in the back. The seat she always sat in with Nate. She looked out the nose-smudged windows. There, just there, she saw him: Nate trotting beside Ricky Sands, trying his level best to keep up with the taller boy's long strides. Ricky said something and elbowed Nate in the side. Nate laughed and glanced back toward the school bus.

He had deserted her.

Gen watched him grow smaller and smaller as the bus left school and boy behind. Her heart was as heavy as the Beam family Bible locked away in her great-grandmother's cedar chest.

She leaned her head against the window and closed her eyes. Why had he gone with Ricky Sands when they always handed out the Turtle Rules together? He knew it was important. And why had he yelled at her and said that thing about acting like a normal person? She was being who she had always been, and he'd always understood. They'd always stuck together through thick and through thin, no matter what.

She gazed into the wide, surprised eyes of Albert Einstein on the back of her pack. She understood advanced physics and the finer points of trigonometry, but she would *never* understand the workings of people's emotions.

Gen's mama set out a plate of cookies and a glass of milk for her daughter. She sat down across the small kitchen table from her and asked what she always did: "How was your day, sugar?" Mrs. Beam folded her hands and waited for the usual complaints about the questionable quality of public education and the lack of edible choices in the cafeteria.

Instead, Gen asked, "Mama, do you believe in luck?"

Mrs. Beam blinked in surprise. She smoothed her dark hair and said, "Why, that's an interesting question, honey. I'm not sure. . . . Your father says everything is God's will and part of God's plan. And my mama said everything happens for a reason. . . ." Her voice trailed off. "On the other hand, it does sometimes seem like some folks are just born lucky and others are born *un*lucky."

"Like Nathaniel," Gen said. Before her mama could answer, she said, "Nathaniel says ever since he got struck by lightning, his luck has changed. He thinks he's gone from unlucky to lucky."

"Hmmm . . . ," Mrs. Beam said.

"I keep telling him there's no such thing as luck, good or bad," she said, without her usual conviction. "Although," she mused, "it is an interesting theory, and it does seem things have been going his way."

"Really?"

"But that could just be self-fulfilling prophecy, couldn't it, Mama? I mean, because he *thinks* he's lucky, he has succeeded more, right?"

"Well, that could be, honey. Maybe he's gotten more self-confidence because he believes his luck has changed, and you and I both know Nate's never had an abundance of self-confidence. But on the other hand, how do you prove the difference between the power of belief and the magic of luck?"

Gen's eyes widened. She jumped up from the table, knocking her chair backward. "That's it, Mama! Why didn't I think of that myself? Every scientific theory must be tested, retested, and proved." She threw her arms around her mother's neck. "You're a genius, Mama!"

CHAPTER 9

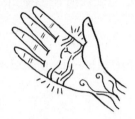

On Friday, the bandages came off once and for all.

"Well," said Dr. Silverstein, "it could look a lot worse, Nate. Those doctors over at the Panama City Hospital know their stuff."

Nate gaped at the marks left behind by the lightning strike. Thin red lines snaked and swirled like vines from his wrist up his skinny forearm.

His grandpa reached out a finger to touch the boy's arm, then thought better of it. "Does it hurt?"

"Not exactly," he said. "Sometimes it feels like bees buzzing under my skin, though."

Dr. Silverstein peered at the outline of the seams of the golf club grip burned forever into Nate's palm. He squinted at two letters below the seams. "Looks like an *L* and a *Y*." He shook his head. "Amazing what lightning will do, isn't it?"

Nate shivered and smiled. "Yes sir."

Grandpa slipped Nate's shirt over his shoulders. "Boy seems to get cold a lot," he said to the doctor. "Even when it's hot outside."

"Not surprised," Dr. Silverstein said as he rubbed a fishy-smelling salve over the scars. "Even though the lightning didn't go through you, it can still play havoc on all the body's systems. You still having bad headaches?" the doctor asked.

Nate was indeed still plagued by headaches (and wished almost every day he hadn't lost his red tennis shoe), but he figured it was a small price to pay for all the good luck he'd had since that fateful day. "No sir," he said. "Hardly ever."

Grandpa reached out his hand to help him off the examining table. He grabbed his grandfather's wrist and climbed down.

Later that day, Nate and his grandfather walked down to the docks to watch the shrimp boats come in from the Gulf to the bay. Paradise Beach was, in fact, a peninsula cradled between the Gulf of Mexico and Apalachicola Bay. Twelve miles long and three miles wide, it stuck out from the mainland like a thumb trying to hitch a ride from a passing hurricane.

Between their trailer and the docks, Nate snapped photos of one pink plastic sandal (child size), one white patent leather shoe with a gold buckle (baby doll size), and a loafer (adult size). A lucky stretch for shoe photos.

Mayor Barnacle Bill sat on the sun-warmed planks, his wet black nose searching the salty, fishy breeze. "Evening, Mayor," Grandpa said with a nod.

Nate sat down next to the mayor and slid an arm around the dog's shoulders.

"Hi, Barney," he said, rubbing the old dog's ears. The mayor gave him a lick on the nose.

The three sat in easy silence, thinking about fish and shoes and the goodness of the day.

After a bit, Mayor Barney rose and shook off his contemplation. Grandpa stood and glanced at his watch. "Reckon it's time we head on over for the town hall meeting." Then he looked at his watch again. "Well, I'll be dipped and fried," he said.

"What is it?"

"My watch," Grandpa said, shaking his head in disbelief. "It's working!"

Which is something watches should do. But Grandpa's watch hadn't worked in the thirteen years since Nate's grandma Jodie had died. Still, he wore that watch because she had given it to him.

Nate remembered feeling the smooth face of the watch beneath his fingers as he held on to his grandpa's wrist in the doctor's office. He smiled up at his grandpa. "That sure is lucky, huh?"

Grandpa shook his head in wonder. "Think Reverend Beam would qualify it as a miracle?" he asked as the mayor escorted them to the town hall.

Paradise Beach's town hall had once been a grand affair with marble floors, tall leaded glass windows, and an elaborate punched-tin ceiling. Rich mahogany handrails sashayed alongside the stairs that had once led to the spacious rooms upstairs. Back when Paradise Beach had been a bustling fishing port and its forests yielded turpentine, this building was the center of a very busy hive.

Now the town hall was a mere shadow of its former self. The marble floors were scratched and dull, and some of the windows were boarded over. The spacious rooms above made a fine home for seagulls and cormorants in the winter. Still, it was a busy place. It not only served as the town hall, but also as the volunteer fire department. Anyone who had cause to hold a monthly meeting held it there, and the cavernous basement was the safest place during a hurricane or tornado — something that gave the old building a measure of comfort and pride.

Nate and his grandfather took seats next to Reverend Beam and Gen. Nate had never seen so many people at a town hall meeting before. Mr. Billy, the unofficial keeper of the town hall (as well as traffic director), brought out more folding chairs.

Nate leaned across his grandfather and said above the noise, "Gen, what the heck are you doing here?" He couldn't remember another time Gen had come to a town council meeting.

Gen held up her Turtle Rules flyers and frowned. "Since you were too busy to help me hand them out, I have to do it here."

A finger of guilt tapped Nate on the shoulder. He had, in fact, left Gen high and dry that afternoon. But he'd hit not one but *two* home runs, and they hadn't even put him in the outfield. He wiggled in his seat with pleasure from the memory.

Councilman Lamprey, flanked on either side by the six other council members, tapped his pen on his water glass. "Can I have your attention, please?"

No one listened.

Nate's grandpa put two fingers to his lips and let out a high, earsplitting whistle. Mayor Barney barked. The room fell silent.

"Thank you, Jonah, Mr. Mayor," Councilman Lamprey said. Ricky Sands's daddy, who sat just to the left of Councilman Lamprey, rolled his eyes.

"Before we begin tonight's meeting, we are fortunate, as always, to have Miss Lillian inspire us with her latest musings." He held out a hand to a tiny woman, no bigger than a minute, clutching a sheaf of papers to her chest.

Miss Lillian skittered tentatively to the front of the room. Her white stockinged legs stuck out like pipe cleaners beneath her faded flowered dress. She ducked her head up and down between her shoulders as she peered out at the faces gathered before her. To Nate, she looked for all the world like one of the little sandpipers down on the beach.

Miss Lillian fluffed her feathers and cleared her throat. Her paper-thin voice quavered as she read "Consider the Improbable Pelican." Her bright eyes darted above the paper trembling in her hand.

> *Oh consider the improbable pelican*
> *as it sails o'er the wind and sea.*
> *His bill doth be too largish for his head;*
> *one might say he lacks a certain symmetry.*
> *He is but an ordinary brown,*
> *he sports no fancy plumage.*
> *His legs art short, his body round;*
> *some might say he looks buffoonish.*

(Nate's teacher, Mr. Peck, groaned.)

> *But, oh! Consider the improbable pelican, dear reader,*
> *as he sails the ocean blue.*
> *He doth glide above the frothy waves, he doth dive*
> > *below the sea.*

He fills his pouch with fish after fish — he's a better

fisherman than you.

The room was silent. Miss Lillian shuffled her papers and then blinked. "That's all," she whispered. Nate clapped enthusiastically; everyone else followed suit politely.

"Thank you as always, Miss Lillian, for giving us much to think about," Councilman Lamprey said to the trembling woman. "Mayor, would you be so kind as to escort Miss Lillian back to her seat?"

The tiny woman scuttled back to her chair clutching her poem and the old dog's collar.

"Now as y'all know, the Billy Bowlegs Festival is just one week away," Councilman Lamprey said. "The prizes are a bit skimpy this year."

"That's because those Rotary folks over in Apalachicola are having their Bounties of the Bay Festival the same durn weekend," someone called from the back. Heads nodded.

"Yeah, they lured away lots of the businesses that usually donate prizes," Coach Hull grumbled.

"Now, now, it's just bad timing they're holding their festival the same weekend as ours," Reverend Beam said. More muttering from the back of the room. Old man Marler snored, his chair tipped back against the wall.

"How about the cash prize for the shrimp boat race, Jonah?" the captain of the *LunaSea* asked.

Nate's grandpa switched his toothpick from one side of his mouth to the other and looked up at the ceiling. He rubbed the back of his sunburned neck. "Well now, I will say I've seen larger donations in my years as grand marshal. What with the economy and a few of the businesses relocating up to Tallahassee . . ." His grandfather trailed off.

Old man Marler woke with a start when his chair tipped forward. "It's those dang astronauts flying around up there, I tell you," he said, blinking his eyes.

"But we still have a week," Grandpa said. "I'll get after y'all who haven't donated to the cash prize, you know I will." Everyone laughed.

"Well, we do have one very generous donor." Councilman Lamprey beamed at Ricky Sands's daddy. "Our good friend and neighbor Melvin Sands has generously donated a brand-new 1992 Ford truck to be raffled off to benefit our fire department."

"Hope you fixed that busted windshield," Sully Punks called out. Everyone laughed. Mr. Sands scowled.

Nate slunk down in his chair. Who knew the first ball he ever hit in his life would fly all the way over to Crystal Sands New and Used Cars?

"We still have plenty of fun prizes for the crab races, oyster shucking, and hush puppy eating contests," Councilman Lamprey assured the crowd.

Chief Brandy, head of the Paradise Beach volunteer fire department, stood. He cleared his throat and said, "I want to remind everyone that, because of the drought, we won't be shooting off any fireworks for the festival. If we're lucky, we can have a few on the Fourth of July."

"Oh, come on, Chief," Mr. Sands said. "A few fireworks won't hurt anything." Everyone knew he sold fireworks as one of his many side businesses.

Chief Brandy stroked his mustache and looked nervously at the heads nodding in agreement. "Well, um, the grasses and sea oats are dry as tinder. All it would take is one spark and the whole beachfront would go up in flames." He looked down at his scuffed shoes.

"We'll just pump water out of the Gulf," Mr. Sands said.

More heads nodded in agreement. Someone called, "Yeah, what's Billy Bowlegs without fireworks?"

"Nobody from out of town will come to the festival without fireworks, and then where will we be? How will we make any money?" Coach Hull asked.

Mutterings of agreement ricocheted around the room. Nate looked up at his grandpa worriedly.

And then, wonder of wonders, Gen stood up. She pushed her glasses up on her nose and raised her hand. The mayor barked. Loud.

The room fell silent.

"Yes, Miss Beam?" Councilman Lamprey said.

Gen took a deep breath. Only Nate, his grandpa, and her daddy were close enough to see the trembling of her knees. In a loud, clear voice, she said, "It's actually a good thing we can't have fireworks."

Councilman Lamprey raised his eyebrows. "Why's that?"

She waved her papers. "Because as you know, the turtles will be here to nest about that time. That's why I brought everyone a copy of the Turtle Rules."

Groans circled the room. "I don't see what those turtles have to do with having fireworks or not," Mr. Sands said.

"The fireworks confuse them," she explained. "As do any other lights near the beach. It's our job to protect them, to care for them. They've been coming to these beaches to lay their eggs for thousands of years. You can count on them" — she shot a look at Nate — "unlike some people I know."

"Those turtles sound pretty stupid if you ask me." Mr. Sands tipped back in his chair and grinned.

"'Those turtles' are more important than the *stupid* money you make off your *stupid* fireworks," Gen snapped.

Mr. Sands shot forward in his chair, his cold eyes fixed on Gen. "Now you look here, girl. . . ."

A storm cloud flashed across Nate's face. He was about to jump to his feet when his grandpa grabbed the back of his T-shirt and pulled him into his seat. "This ain't your fight, boy," his grandpa whispered.

Reverend Beam slowly stood and put his arm around his daughter. Although he smiled, his eyes were not a bit warm. "I think what my daughter, however inelegantly, is trying to say is that our natural resources are far more valuable than any tourist dollars we might see." Heads nodded in agreement.

Picking up steam, the good reverend continued, "We are purely *blessed* in Paradise Beach with the good Lord's bountiful beauty and wonder. We are stewards of this paradise, charged with protecting her."

"Amen!" Miss Lillian called in a loud whisper.

"Save your sermon for Sunday, preacher," Mr. Sands said.

"Yeah," someone called. "We don't need preaching, we need those tourist dollars."

"Amen to that," the town postmistress said.

"We need a lucky break for once," Coach Hull said.

"Rowoof! Rowroof!" the mayor barked.

"Gentlemen!" A voice like the trumpets of Gabriel rang out. The room fell silent.

A substantial woman, a woman who suffered no fools, rose from her chair in the corner of the room. Men and women who fought the elements out on the sea to make a living, folks who bossed other folks around and handled large sums of money, trembled in their seats. Everyone who had stood sat down, including Reverend Beam and Gen.

"Oh yes, Mrs. Belk, please do speak," Councilman Lamprey stammered. "We of course want to hear you weigh in — I mean, as it were . . ."

The woman held up her hand. Everyone held their breath. "As president of the Paradise Beach Garden and Beautification League, I speak for all of us when I say we support the fire department's decision to *not* have fireworks at this year's Billy Bowlegs Festival." The other members of the Garden and Beautification League nodded in agreement. Mrs. Belk looked slowly around the room, daring anyone to defy her. No one did. Almost every woman in Paradise Beach belonged to the Garden and Beautification League, including Councilman Lamprey's and Mr. Sands's wives. Everyone in town knew better than to make enemies of the Paradise Beach Garden and Beautification League.

Mrs. Belk, whose husband was the president of Gulf Coast Bank and Trust, crossed one arm over the other. "And, I might add, I personally agree with Reverend Beam. You cannot put a price on the God-given beauty of this place. It is our greatest resource."

"And we expect *everyone* to donate generously at our kissing booth at the festival," a small woman much resembling a possum added, from the back of the crowd.

"Yes, dear," Councilman Lamprey said.

After Nate helped Gen hand out copies of the Turtle Rules to each and every person at the town meeting, he looked for his grandpa. He heard thunder rumbling somewhere off in the distance and his head hurt like the dickens.

Finally, he spotted his grandfather, cornered by two other charter boat captains. The two captains did not look happy.

"What're you doing, Jonah, to bribe all these tourists onto the *Sweet Jodie*? You paying their hotel bills? Offering them free dinner or something?" the captain of the *SeaBiscuit* asked in a not entirely friendly way.

Nate's grandpa laughed uneasily and pulled on his white ponytail.

"Yeah," said the captain of the *LunaSea*. "Seems like you got some kind of game going, Jonah."

Grandpa switched his toothpick from one side of his mouth to the other and shrugged. "No game, Rusty. Just luck, I reckon."

"Yeah, well, your good luck is taking business away from —"

Before the captain could finish, Nate tugged on his grandfather's arm. "Hey, Grandpa."

Grandpa pulled the boy to him. "Speaking of lucky!"

The two disgruntled captains smiled and shook their heads. "Truer words were never spoken," the captain of the *SeaBiscuit* said.

Lightning flashed outside the tall windows. Nate shook beneath his grandfather's hand and let out a tiny moan.

"We best be getting home," Grandpa said. "The boy's not a big fan of thunderstorms, and we walked over here."

"I'll give y'all a lift," the *LunaSea*'s captain said.

"Don't want to put you to any trouble," Grandpa said. Lightning flashed again. Nate shook like a frightened puppy. "But if you're sure it won't put you out . . ."

"No trouble at all," the captain said. As they dashed to his car, he grabbed Nate's lightning-scarred hand. His weatherworn palm mashed right up against the *L* and *Y* burned into Nate's palm. "Maybe some of your good luck will rub off on me," the captain said over the rising wind.

The next day and for many days after, the captain of the *LunaSea* had more business than he knew what to do with.

CHAPTER 10

One luck-filled week later, Nate fairly sailed through the Sweet Magnolia RV and Trailer Park on his bike as he made his way over to Gen's. Tonight was the kickoff to the weekend-long Billy Bowlegs Festival, culminating in the Blessing of the Fleet. All week, the town had been getting ready to celebrate the founder of Paradise Beach, the pirate Billy Bowlegs. All weekend the town would be abuzz with arts and crafts, shrimp boat races, crab races, reenactments of the day Billy Bowlegs washed up on the shores of what was now Paradise Beach, and, of course, one long, continuous fish fry.

He had never been to the carnival, with its rides and cotton candy and games. Grandpa was always busy getting the boat ready for the Blessing of the Fleet, and Gen hated crowds. But this year, Nate Harlow was going to the carnival with Ricky Sands and a whole mess of his equally popular friends.

He smiled into the cloud-studded sky and fingered the lucky rabbit's foot in his pocket.

He found Gen reading on the back porch of The Church of the One True Redeemer and Everlasting Light, Mercy and Goodness curled in her lap.

"Hey Gen," he said, parking his bike and mounting the steps to the porch. "You want to come with me to watch them set up the carnival?"

She barely glanced up from her book. "Too hot."

"Come on, Gen," he pleaded. "It'll be fun, it'll be different."

"You know I don't like 'different,'" Gen snapped, hard as a turtle.

Nate sighed. "How long you going to stay mad at me?"

Pink splotches bloomed on her neck and face. She pushed her glasses up on her nose. "I'm not mad. I don't care if you go to that stupid carnival with Ricky Sands and his merry band of philistines."

Nate pinched his nose and pitched his voice high. "I beg to differ," he said in an almost perfect imitation of Gen and one of her favorite comebacks.

He watched for a smile. He knew for a fact he was the only one who could get away with imitating her and not get socked in the belly.

No smile came. Without looking at him, she said, "We need to go to our dune and watch for the loggerheads." She scratched the chin of the tabby named Mercy. "My calculations of the currents and ocean temperatures and tides show they should start coming in any night now. Plus, tonight is the first night of the full moon."

Nate frowned. "I've never been to the carnival, Gen. I want to do what the other kids are doing for once."

An awkward silence grew between the two friends.

Finally, he said, "I'll go down to the beach with you another night."

"Do what you want," she said, not looking at him. Goodness glared at Nate from Gen's lap. And if the cats had not curled up on the book she had been reading, he might have wondered at the title: *Test Your Luck*.

That night, Nate fingered the money in his pocket his grandpa had given him for the carnival. "Don't spend it all at once," Grandpa said. "And stay away from those games of luck. They're run by riffraff. They're just out to steal your money."

But Grandpa's words did not find a place of prominence in his mind, because Nate's mind and nose and eyes were filled with the glory of the carnival. Flashing, spinning lights! The smell of popcorn, peanuts, sugar, and fry grease! Everywhere he looked, his eyes took in the colors of brightly painted rides and all sorts of prizes dangling from the tent eaves. Everybody from miles around crammed into Billy Bowlegs Park.

Ricky Sands jabbed him in the ribs with his elbow. "Better shut your mouth, Sparky, or a fly will get in," he said.

He snapped his mouth shut and trotted behind Ricky and Connor and a bunch of other boys. They shoved their way over to the Tilt-A-Whirl. Nate's heart bounded into his throat as he climbed into the half-cup seat with Ricky and Connor. By the end of the ride, it wasn't just his heart squirming in his throat.

"You're green as seaweed," Connor said, laughing.

"If you're gonna puke, get away from me!" one of the other boys said.

Nate swallowed hard and shook his head. "I'm okay." He could just see Gen rolling her eyes.

"Lookit!" Ricky said. "They got the Monster Masher here!"

Nate forced himself to look where Ricky pointed. A tall, silver, rocket-shaped ride shot screaming passengers high into the air, then jerked them back down again. Up and down, up and down the screaming, crying, strapped-in, unable-to-get-away passengers flew. His legs quivered like jellyfish.

"Awesome," the boys said in reverent voices.

Nate closed his eyes and pictured Gen atop their dune — the tallest dune on Paradise Beach — the sea oats rattling in the wind, watching the water's edge shimmering in the moonlight for signs of the turtles. Right then, he wished like anything he were right there beside her.

Ricky thumped him so hard on his back, he almost fell to the ground. "This'll make a man out of you."

Nate sighed and trailed behind the boys as they made their way through the crowd over to the Monster Masher. He watched as the freed passengers staggered and wobbled from the ride. Coach Hull smiled weakly at the boys, then threw up behind the bushes. Nate felt the corn dog he'd eaten rise up from his stomach in sympathy.

"Whoa!" Connor said. "Did you see Coach?" The boys laughed and poked and made retching sounds, which did not help Nate's efforts to keep his corn dog where it belonged.

He shuffled forward in line, shuddering and shaking. Ricky and Connor bought their tickets and raced over to the giant, heaving machine.

"How old are you, kid?"

Nate opened his eyes and looked up past a big, round belly to the cigar jutting from the mouth of the ticket taker. "Eleven, sir," he said.

The man shifted his cigar to the other side of his mouth and tapped a cardboard hand with his cane. "See this here?"

Nate nodded.

"You gotta be this tall to go on this ride." He shoved Nate over to the hand, which hovered a good half foot above his head. "Too short," the cigar man declared to one and all. "Can't go on this ride, kid." In a lower voice he said, "Sorry."

Nate shrugged and waved to Ricky and the other boys. They laughed and shook their heads as they were strapped in one by one.

He forced himself to walk away in a feet-dragging-with-disappointment kind of way. What he really wanted to do was skip. For the first time in his life, being short had brought him luck!

Nate wandered over to the ring toss.

"Five rings, five chances to win, folks! Only a dollar to win one of these fabulous prizes!"

Coach Hull, still a little green around the gills, tossed one, then two, three, then four rings into the air. Each landed neat as you please over the neck of the milk bottles. He rubbed his hands together and winked at a beaming Miss Trundle. "The next one's for you, Trudy."

He tossed the fifth wooden ring. It wobbled and wavered in the air. Nate held his breath. Coach Hull and Miss Trundle held their breath. The ring fell with a tiny *clink*.

Miss Trundle clapped her chubby hands together. "Oh my, Don! You're so talented!"

Coach grinned and puffed out his chest. "Pick out your prize, Trudy," he said.

Nate was not a bit surprised when Miss Trundle chose a large pink cat with diamond sparkly eyes. She hugged it to her pillowy chest.

"How about you, young fella?" the man behind the counter said. "You want to try? It's just a dollar."

Coach Hull frowned. "Nate, you're not exactly good at this sort of thing."

He looked at the wooden rings the man twirled on his arm. The man grinned. "Might be your lucky night, huh, boy?"

Lucky. Nate looked at the *L* and *Y* burned into the palm of his hand. He rubbed his thumb over the rabbit's foot in his pocket.

He stepped up and slapped his dollar bill on the sticky wooden table. "Yes sir, it just might be." And it was.

Every ring he tossed fairly sang its way to the nearest bottle and settled around its shoulder with a happy sigh.

And he was not just lucky at the ring toss. Oh no, his

hand knew exactly which yellow rubber ducky bobbing through the circular creek had the best prize numbers. He guessed right down to the ounce the weight of the fat lady. By the time Nate made it to the baseball throw, a crowd trailed behind him, including Ricky Sands and his gang.

Jinx Malloy stood before the table, smacking the baseball in her hand. She narrowed her eyes at the rows of miniature clowns standing straight as soldiers seven feet away.

"Alls you got to do, little lady, is knock down four of those fellas," a tattooed man said as he took her money.

Jinx glared at the man. She pulled her cap down tight on her head and flipped her braids behind her shoulders. She spit on the ground and let loose a throw that could have gone all the way to Wewahitchka. The clowns didn't stand a chance.

"That's one," the tattooed man cried. He tossed Jinx another ball. "Think you can knock down another one?"

She did. She knocked down the next one too. The crowd clapped. "Come on, Jinx," Nate said. "Just one more."

Jinx wound up her arm tight as a tick and grinned. She took aim at one particularly goofy clown and let the ball fly.

The ball smacked the clown right in its grinning face. *Thwack!* Half the clown's hat popped off. The clown wobbled and tilted. The crowd clapped.

But the clown did not fall. It popped back up, listing a bit to one side.

"Aw, tough luck, honey," the tattooed man said, grinning.

"It's rigged!" Jinx said. "I hit that stupid clown hard enough to break his face!"

The tattooed man ignored her outburst. "Who's next?" he asked the crowd.

Ricky Sands strutted up to the table and handed over his money. "I'll show you how it's done," he said, winking at Jinx.

And it looked like he would too. He knocked down the first and second clowns with barely a thought. Ricky grinned at Jinx and wound up for his third toss. *Thwack!* The ball hit a clown square in its grinning mouth. It didn't budge.

The crowd gasped. Ricky stared in disbelief. "No way," Connor called from the sidelines. "That clown should have gone down."

"Yeah, it's rigged," someone cried.

The tattooed man glared at the grumbling crowd. "You pays your money, you takes your chances," he said. "Who's next?" he asked, surveying the crowd with narrowed eyes.

Ricky grabbed Nate by the shoulders and shoved him toward the table. "He is."

The man looked at the small boy standing before him, his arms full of stuffed animals, lightsabers, and a giant inflatable hammer. The man grinned. "Looks like you're the big winner tonight," he said. "Care to try your luck here?"

Nate hesitated. Maybe he'd used up all his luck for one night. Was luck like that?

But then he saw it, hanging in the rafters among the stuffed bears and giraffes, the plastic rifles and guitars: a magnificent bright blue sombrero with red trim. His grandpa had had one almost like it years ago until it was lost in a tornado (yes, that same tornado that'd snatched up Nate's hound dog). Oh, he could just imagine the smile on his grandpa's face if he won that sombrero.

"I reckon," he said.

Murmurs rippled through the crowd. Bobby Louder and all the little Louders clapped and chanted, "Spark-*y*! Spark-*y*!"

Nate handed the stuffed animals to Jinx and the rest of his booty to Ricky Sands. He handed his last dollar bill to the tattooed man. The man handed him a ball. "Whenever you're ready," he said.

Nate looked at the rows of grinning clowns. The baseball grew warmer and warmer in his hand. He took aim and threw.

"That's one down," the tattooed man cried. He handed Nate the next ball.

"That's two down."

And then, "That's *three* down." The tattooed man spit a stream of chewing tobacco into the dirt. He studied Nate through narrowed eyes.

Applause peppered the evening air. "Come on, Nate," Jinx called.

He glanced her way and smiled. With the fourth ball in his hand, he took aim at the clown with half a hat. If he didn't know better, he could've sworn it tried to hide behind one of the other clowns.

"No you don't," he said under his breath.

He let loose the ball. It shot straight as an arrow right smack into the face of that clown. It fell backward, but then, just like before, bounced right back up.

"No way," the crowd cried. The tattooed man grinned.

But that ball wasn't done. Oh no. It smacked against the canvas backdrop, ricocheted forward, and hit that clown in the back of the head. This time, when the clown fell, it did not get up.

Bobby Louder and all the little Louders jumped up and down yelling, "Nate won! Nate won!"

Coach Hull grinned. "I taught him all he knows," he said, and Miss Trundle said over and over, "Such a nice boy." Jinx Malloy raised her hand for a high five, which Nate happily slapped.

He turned to the tattooed man. "I'd like my prize, please."

The tattooed man scowled. "Pick one," he snapped.

He pointed to the sombrero. "That one," he declared. He couldn't wait to get home and give his grandpa this hat.

Ricky Sands raised Nate's arms high in the air and shook them. "You're the champ, Sparky!"

The sleeves of Nate's shirt slid down his arms.

The crowd gasped.

"Whoa," someone behind him said. "Would you look at that." The crowd stared wide-eyed at the lightning marks twisting and winding their way around and up his arm.

He dropped his arms.

The littlest Louder stepped up and touched Nate's scarred arm. "I want some of that luck," he said.

"I don't think —"

Before he could finish, the rest of the Louders and even some of the bigger kids surrounded him. They shoved their dollar bills into his hands. "Win a prize for me!" they demanded.

And Nate did. Turn after turn, dollar after dollar, he knocked the stuffing out of those clowns. Within fifteen minutes, the tattooed man didn't have a single prize left.

The bigger kids slapped him on the back, the girls smiled shyly, and the little kids pulled and climbed on his arms and legs. He felt ten feet and eight inches tall.

The tattooed man pushed the crowd away, shoved his face close to Nate's, and growled, "How did you do that, kid?"

He shook his head. "I don't know what you mean."

"Some kind of trick up your sleeve?" He grabbed Nate by the arms and shook him, like he was trying to shake something loose. "Where you hiding it?" The blue sombrero fell to the ground.

Just when he thought the man was going to shake his arms out of their sockets, Miss Trundle smacked the tattooed man in the back of his head with her sizable purse. "Get your hands off him, you hooligan!"

Coach Hull rushed in. "Yes, unhand the boy."

Miss Trundle shepherded Nate away from the tattooed man, sweeping up the sombrero with her other hand.

But not before he heard the man yell, "You *stole* from me, kid. You stole! You haven't seen the last of me!"

CHAPTER 11

Much to Nate's eternal relief, the carnival had packed up and moved on by the next day. Still, the ice in the tattooed man's eyes and the cold fury in his words — "You haven't seen the last of me!" — sent a shiver through Nate's body.

Nate raced down to the docks on his bike to find his grandpa. Grandpa himself would not be in the shrimp boat race. The *Sweet Jodie* was, after all, a deep sea fishing boat. But Grandpa's grandpa had been the one to start the races many years ago, before Paradise Beach had paved roads and electricity. Jonah Harlow, like his father before him, was the unofficial grand marshal of the shrimp boat races. He alone judged the boats' decorations and called the winner of the race. Grandpa often said, on that one day out of the year, he was a big fish in a very small pond.

Nate spotted his grandpa's white ponytail and blue straw

sombrero. He grinned, remembering the night before when he gave his grandpa the hat.

"Grandpa!" he hollered.

Someone grabbed him by the shoulder. *"You."*

Nate's stomach slid down to his toes. He squirmed and twisted away from the hand.

"You're Jonah Harlow's boy." Nate squinted up at the face in front of him. It was not the face of the tattooed man. It was the sun-weathered face of Big Jim Sands, Ricky Sands's grandpa. "I hear from my grandson you were just about the luckiest boy there ever was at the carnival last night."

"Yes sir, I reckon I was lucky." He looked again for his grandpa.

Big Jim clamped a hand on Nate's shoulder and pinched it like a crab. He smiled. "How about you ride with me on my boat in the race? I could use a little extra luck. Kind of like all that luck your granddaddy's been having." It did not escape his notice that Big Jim's smile resided only on his lips and around his chewing tobacco–stained teeth and did not rise to the storm-gray eyes.

But before he could answer, another shrimper grabbed

his other arm and pulled. "This boy don't want to ride in your smelly old rust bucket," he said. "You come on now, Nate, and ride with me."

"Now just a doggone minute," Big Jim growled, pulling Nate's right arm none too gently.

"You listen here, Big Jim, this boy's riding with me." The other shrimper tugged on Nate's left arm. Nate knew exactly how the wishbone from the Thanksgiving turkey felt.

Just as Nate thought he would surely be pulled in two, his grandpa clamped his hands on each man's wrist, fingers pressing into the flesh. Hard. Hands dropped away from Nate. Grandpa pulled the boy to him.

"I do appreciate y'all being so generous, offering my boy a ride on your shrimp boats," Grandpa said, in an even voice that could have frozen salt water. "Funny how you've never done that before."

The two men studied their shoes. It was true: Nate's reputation for being unlucky had kept him from ever being invited to ride with a shrimper during the race like most kids had.

Grandpa steered Nate through the crowds spilling from the docks onto the street. He patted his shoulder. "You okay?"

"Yes sir," he said. "It was strange, though."

Grandpa held his blue straw sombrero against a frisky breeze. "People get odd notions in their heads." Grandpa picked him up and parked him on top of the spreading wings of a huge bronze pelican. "You wait here and keep out of trouble. I need to go check the last entries. Oh, and Gen's looking for you."

Nate gazed at the shrimp boats rocking gently in the bay against the docks. Some were outfitted to look like pirate ships, with black flags bearing the skull and crossbones and fake cannons. Others sported colorful streamers from the wide arms of the boats and Christmas lights. One boat was all made up to look like a dragon, another's nets were strung with hundreds of balloons. Nate smiled. It was nice to see these homely, some would even say downright ugly boats looking fine.

"Ladies and gentlemen," Grandpa's voice boomed over the loudspeaker from his place up on the judge's platform. "Welcome to the fifty-third annual Billy Bowlegs Festival and shrimp boat race!"

Everyone clapped and cheered.

Something small and white underneath a bench caught Nate's eye. A tiny white leather shoe — baby doll size — just like the one he'd taken a picture of last week. What luck! If he could reunite the pair of shoes, wouldn't that be something? Gen had always said the chances of that happening were . . . well, he couldn't remember, but not very likely. "I'll find her and show her," he said, scanning the crowd for his friend.

"Captains," Nate's grandpa commanded from his post on high. "Start your engines!" Twelve shrimp boat engines coughed and chugged to life. The crowd whooped and hollered. Off to one side, all by herself, he saw Gen. One hand shaded her eyes from the sun while the other worried an eyebrow. He cupped his hands around his mouth. "Gen! Hey, Gen! Over here!"

A hand grasped Nate's flip-flop. *"You,"* a voice hissed from below.

He looked down. All the spit in his mouth turned dry as dust. A hand, a hand with long yellow fingernails, a hand attached to an arm covered with tattoos, clutched his foot.

He jerked his foot back like it'd been struck by lightning. He jumped off the giant pelican. The tattooed man grabbed for him.

"Captains!" Grandpa commanded again. "On your mark."

"You *stole* from me, boy," the tattooed man snarled.

"I don't know what you mean," Nate cried, ducking between the giant pelican's spindly legs.

"Nathaniel! Over here!" Gen waved both her hands.

"Get set," Grandpa bellowed through the loudspeaker.

"You owe me," the man said, grabbing hold of Nate's shirt-sleeve. He spun away, leaving his shirt and one flip-flop behind.

"Go!" Grandpa cried.

And Nate went. He ran as fast as his one-flip-flopped foot could carry him. He pushed and bumped his way through the crowd, which brought a warning holler from Mr. Billy, the town's unofficial crowd controller. He glanced back over his shoulder. The tattooed man was gaining fast.

"Lord help me," Nate whimpered. He fixed his eyes on the very last shrimp boat pulling away from the docks. He took a deep breath and pushed off the dock hard with his legs. He rose, arms flapping in the air, legs pedaling as hard as they could. He landed with a *thud* and a *splat* on the wooden deck of the boat.

There he lay, the thrum of the boat engine against his ear and the cheers of the crowd becoming just the tiniest bit faint. He felt the boat shudder and pick up speed.

"Nate? Is that you?"

Slowly, he sat up. Chum Bailey frowned down at him.

He blinked in the sun. "Hey, Chum, how you doing?" he said, as if he dropped onto shrimp boats on a regular basis — which he surely did not.

Chum looked to the left, then to the right, and finally heavenward. "Where the heck did you come from?"

Nate stood unsteadily and looked back toward the docks. The tattooed man grew smaller and smaller. Nate shivered in the sea breeze as the *Bay Leaf* picked up steam. Long white strips of tattered bed sheets and old T-shirts streamed and fluttered like feathers from the *Bay Leaf*'s outrigging.

Which is not to say this particular shrimp boat streaked through the water with the grace and speed of a dolphin, nor did it skim the water like a seagull. No, the *Bay Leaf* was a boat given to lollygagging. It meandered this way and that depending on the whims and curiosities of its captain, Rem Bailey.

Chum touched Nate's shoulder. "You're shaking like a leaf. Let's get you up in the cabin with Daddy." They picked their way around ropes and pulleys and nets to the squat glass cabin in the front.

"Hey, Daddy," Chum said, pushing Nate through the doorway. "This here's my friend, Nate Harlow, from school. I told you about him."

A surprisingly small man smiled from the captain's chair. "Welcome aboard, Nate. You're Jonah Harlow's boy, right? The one got struck by lightning?"

"Yes sir," he said.

Chum's daddy stuck his hand out. "Proud to meet you."

Nate reached out to take the man's hand, then stopped. The hand was missing all but its thumb and pinky finger, like the pincers of a crab.

Rem Bailey withdrew his hand. "The perils of a shrimper's life," he said, turning his attention back to the bay.

Nate's ears reddened. "Yes sir," he mumbled.

"Looks like we're drawing up to the *Barnacle*, Daddy," Chum called. He hung his head out the side window of the cabin like a dog hanging out a car window, a big grin plastered to his face.

The *Bay Leaf* sallied forth, chugging and stuttering.

"Y'all ever won the race?" Nate asked.

Chum shrugged. "Naw," he said. "We never finished

anything but last. It's almost always the *Dixie Queen*, the Sandses' boat, or the *Miss Lori* that wins."

"Then why do y'all enter if you always finish last?"

Chum shrugged. "My daddy says one of these days Lady Luck will smile on us and we'll win." Chum picked at a piece of flaking paint. "Sure wish it'd be this year," he said, mostly to himself. "We could use the money. Mama's had to work extra shifts over at the Piggly Wiggly in Apalachicola, so she's hardly ever home."

A gray-and-white-striped cat appeared out of nowhere and rubbed against Nate's legs, making him start.

Chum reached down and picked up the cat in his big hands. "This is Mr. Bowditch." Chum took one of the cat's white paws in his hand and waved it at Nate. "Say hi to my friend, Nate."

Nate waved back at the cat.

"Looks like you're missing a flip-flop," Chum pointed out.

"Dang!"

All those single shoes and sandals and boots he had given a home to, had taken pictures of, and now here he was with just one shoe. Again. He figured this is what his teacher, Mr. Peck, would call an irony.

He sighed. "Well, I might as well take a picture of the one I got left." He reached into his pocket for his camera, where it always was, but his pocket was empty. "Cripes!" he cried. "Where's my camera?"

He dashed to the back of the boat where he had landed. No camera. His eyes searched the boat's frothy wake. No luck.

"What are you looking for?" Chum asked.

"My camera," Nate mumbled. "I need to take a picture of my flip-flop because it's . . . well . . ."

"That's too bad. I never had a camera, but I do have two shoes."

Just then, the engine of the *Bay Leaf* coughed and gagged like it had a giant hair ball in its throat. *Gack! Gack!*

And then, silence.

"Oh lordy," Rem Bailey said, sprinting to the back of the boat.

Chum and his daddy stood over the engine compartment shaking their heads.

"Looks bad, Daddy," Chum said, touching the man's shoulder.

"Yes, Charles, you're right about that." He banged the top

of the engine with a wrench and wiggled a wire. "I reckon we're not going to win again this year."

A pelican landed on top of the captain's cabin. It spread its brown wings wide and held them aloft in the sun to dry. The cat rubbed against Nate's legs.

Nate jumped again, stumbled into a coil of ropes, and fell forward, his hand banging against the engine.

The engine hiccupped. The engine sneezed. And then the engine burst to life.

"Whoa, Daddy!" Chum crowed.

Rem Bailey yipped with joy, dashed back to the cabin, and grabbed the wheel. "Hang on to your hats, boys," he called above the mighty thrum of the engine. "Looks like we're back in the race!"

And indeed they were. The *Bay Leaf* fairly flew over the waves. Dolphins raced just ahead of the bow and played in the wide wake of the boat. The pelican squawked from the top of the captain's cabin.

The *Bay Leaf* scampered past the *Urchin*, sashayed around the *Fortuna* and the *LunaSea*, Rem Bailey honking his horn and the boys waving to the astonished crews as they passed.

The little shrimp boat dug in and galloped ahead. "Look, Daddy," Chum called. "There's the *Miss Lori* up ahead."

Rem Bailey stuck his head out the cabin window and grinned into the wind. "Thar she blows!" he said, laughing.

And thar she went. They left the crew of the *Miss Lori* bobbing and rocking in their wake.

"What boat's that up ahead?" Nate asked, squinting at the back of the proud, shining boat racing ahead in the distance.

"That," said Chum in a reverent voice, "is the *Dixie Queen*. They win almost every year."

In no time, the little boat closed the distance. The bow of the *Bay Leaf* all but nosed the stern of the *Dixie Queen*, then drew up alongside.

Nate grinned and waved. "Hey, Ricky, hey, Mr. Sands."

Chum held up the cat's paw and waved it. "Say hello, Mr. Bowditch."

Ricky Sands's mouth dropped open wide as a pelican's pouch. Mr. Sands shook his fist and yelled something that would have gotten Nate's mouth washed out with soap.

"Better close your mouth, Ricky," Nate called across the sound of the engines. "A fish might jump in."

And with that, the *Bay Leaf* leapt ahead of the *Dixie Queen* and raced toward the finish line — a bright ribbon of red stretched between two buoys.

Nate could see his grandpa up in the judge's stand waving two orange flags. The crowds along the docks clapped and hooted and chanted over and over, louder and louder, "*Bay Leaf! Bay Leaf! Bay Leaf!*"

He and Chum pounded their fists on the bow of the boat, and Rem Bailey jumped up and down on top of the captain's cabin. "Go! Go! Go!" they all chanted. The *Bay Leaf* sailed through the finish line, the broken red ribbon fluttering in the breeze.

Nate and Chum and his daddy jumped up and down and danced until the boat about tipped over. Chum picked up his daddy and hollered, "We won, Daddy, we won!" And then he picked up Nate and swung him back and forth like the clapper of a bell. "We won! We won!"

The *Bay Leaf* strutted up to the docks, proud as proud could be.

Everyone cheered as Nate's grandpa cracked a bottle of real champagne over the humble bow of the *Bay Leaf*. He presented the Baileys with a trophy and a check for one thousand dollars. "Drinks are on me!" Rem Bailey cried, holding up the check. And everyone cheered and clapped again.

Rem Bailey pumped Nate's hand with a reverence usually reserved for Father Donovan. "You got the Midas touch, boy. The Midas touch."

"I didn't have anything to do with it," Nate said, pulling his hunched shoulders back and smiling.

"The heck you didn't," Rem Bailey said. Turning to the crowd, he said, "All I know is, that engine was deader than dead until he touched it."

Nate expected everyone to laugh. Instead, some folks nodded in agreement. Others studied him like something shiny half buried in the sand.

For the rest of the day, kids pestered Nate to touch their crab so they'd win the crab race, grown men begged him to sit by them during the oyster shucking contest, and the ladies of the Paradise Island Garden and Beautification League insisted he be one of the kissees at their kissing booth.

By the afternoon, Nate was worn out.

He tugged on his grandpa's hand. "I'm going to head over to Gen's, Grandpa."

"I'm ready to leave too," Grandpa said. "And I got to be back up here at the crack of dawn for the Blessing of the Fleet." He took the boy's hand in his and they walked across the park together.

As they got to the far end of Billy Bowlegs Park, they saw a bright red Ford truck with gleaming hubcaps parked on the grass. Above it a banner read WIN ME FOR A DOLLAR! Grandpa cut a beeline over to the truck. He shook his head as he admired it tip to tail. "Sure is a pretty thing. Makes my old Alfred look like he's ready for the junkyard."

"Only costs you a dollar to buy a raffle ticket," Chief Brandy said. "It's for a good cause."

Grandpa dug around in his pocket and pulled out a dollar bill. He handed it to Nate. "Might as well give it a try, huh, boy?"

"Yes sir," Nate said. He handed Chief Brandy the dollar with his scarred hand.

CHAPTER 12

"Ha!" Nate crowed. "Double sixes *again*! How many times in a row is that, Gen? Huh?" He held up his hand for a high five, even though he knew Gen never, ever gave high fives.

Gen took off her glasses and pinched the bridge of her nose. "Too many," she mumbled. She thumbed through *Test Your Luck*. "Let's try another test."

Rain tapped against the stained glass window in the sanctuary of The Church of the One True Redeemer and Everlasting Light. Nate leaned his back against the pulpit, glad to be away from the crowds of people down at the festival. It wouldn't be so bad, he thought, if they didn't all want something from him.

Gen shuffled a deck of cards and fanned them out before Nate, facedown. "Pick one," she said.

He pulled out the ace of spades.

She shuffled the deck again. "Pick another one."

The ace of hearts slid into his fingers slick as a whistle.

Gen shook her head, shuffled the deck three times, and said, "Pick one with your eyes closed."

He squeezed his eyes shut tight and drew the ace of diamonds.

"Impossible," she said.

For the next hour, Gen threw every test in the book at Nate. And every single time, he was lucky. She closed the book and studied him for a good long while — long enough that he squirmed under her gaze.

"Fascinating," she said, tapping her pencil against her knee. "The lighting strike — *theoretically* — could have reversed certain magnetic fields in your body."

"Huh?" Nate said.

"Of course, that would assume a magnetic field of *unluck-iness* before the lightning strike," she mused. "Which I, for one, find hard to believe."

"But, Gen, how else can you explain it?"

"There is that 'law of attraction' hokum that says you attract into your life whatever you think about. I've always written that off as wishful thinking," she said.

He threw his hands heavenward in exasperation. "Jeez, Gen, you have to believe in *something*." Before Gen could give her usual reply, Nate leaned forward and whispered, "You come to the Blessing of the Fleet in the morning. My grand-daddy bought a raffle ticket for that brand-new 1992 Ford pickup truck they're raffling off."

"So?"

"*So*," he said, leaning in closer, "*I* gave Chief Brandy the dollar bill and took the ticket *with my burned hand*."

Squabbling, squealing voices filled the household above.

"It's mine!"

"No it's not, it's *mine!*"

"If my granddaddy wins that truck, will you believe in me?"

Gen opened her mouth to say something, then snapped it shut. She plucked at one eyebrow, then the other, and nodded her head.

Nate sighed. "I sure wish I hadn't lost my shoe and camera today, though. That's not so lucky." He had looked all down by the docks where he'd lost them, and even waded out into the water among the seaweed and floating fish heads to see if they ended up under the docks. No luck.

Gen shook her head. "I've never understood your obsession with lost shoes."

He shrugged. "It's not *lost* shoes, it's *finding* just one shoe in all these weird places. *Just one.* It's a mystery."

She snorted. "It's not a mystery, just careless people, that's all."

Nate's brow furrowed with concentration. "All these years, I've been collecting those single shoes, taking pictures of them, hoping I'd find the other dropped shoe and bring them back together. And now I've lost shoes twice in the last three weeks. It's weird."

The sun was just barely showing its face the next morning when the residents of Paradise Beach gathered on the docks for the Blessing of the Fleet. Gulls and pelicans fluffed their feathers against the morning chill. Ten yards out, the slick backs and dorsal fins of dolphins shone in the new light.

Nate and his grandpa stood on the front deck of the *Sweet Jodie*. Grandpa sipped a cup of coffee while Nate blew on his hot chocolate. "Looks like a good turnout," Grandpa said. "Folks must be feeling frisky this morning."

Father Donovan, Pastor Jimmy, Rabbi Levine, and the good Reverend Beam stood resplendent in robes and pressed suits. Years ago, only Father Donovan blessed the fleets to ensure a safe and bountiful season, a tradition begun centuries before among the mostly Catholic fishing communities of the Mediterranean. But times being what they'd been (hard) for the last number of years, the community agreed they needed to cover all ecumenical bases.

The sun climbed the horizon. Councilman Lamprey mounted the steps to the makeshift stage with Mayor Barney by his side.

"Good morning, everyone. Welcome to the fifty-third annual Paradise Beach Blessing of the Fleet."

"Aroof! Roof! Roow!" said the mayor.

"Thank you, Mayor, and thank you to everyone for coming out on this fine morning." Nate's heart lifted as a squadron of pelicans skimmed over the glassy water.

"As always, we come together this morning to bless the fleets of brave fishermen —"

"And *women*," Jinx Malloy called from the bow of her mother's charter boat, the *Athena*.

"And women," Councilman Lamprey amended. "These good and brave folks who depend on the vagaries of the weather and the sea for their living, we wish them safe passage and bountiful catches."

The councilman motioned to the four clergy. "In just a minute, I'll invite these gentlemen up to give the blessing. After they're done, there'll be a pancake breakfast over in the park put on by our own Rotary Club. Oh, and y'all don't forget, we'll be drawing the winning raffle ticket for that new Ford pickup truck at ten this morning." Applause and cheers scattered the gulls.

Nate tugged on his grandpa's arm. "You've got the ticket, don't you?"

Grandpa patted his shirt pocket. "Right here. Although I don't think I have much chance of winning."

Nate wasn't too sure either, after losing his flip-flop and camera.

Father Donovan mounted the steps, followed by Pastor Jimmy, Rabbi Levine, and Reverend Beam. The crowd grew quiet.

The four men closed their eyes and bowed their heads. Father Donovan raised his arms, the gold-trimmed white sleeves of his cassock sliding down his sunburned arms. "Most gracious Lord, who numbered among your apostles the fishermen Peter, Andrew, James, and John, we pray you to consecrate these boats to righteous work in your name. Guide the captain at her helm. So prosper her voyages that an honest living may be made."

"Amen to that," Grandpa said.

"Watch over her passengers and crew," Pastor Jimmy added.

"And bring them to a safe return, *Mechayeh Hakol*," Rabbi Levine continued.

"And may the blessing of God Almighty, the Father, the Son, and the Holy Spirit," Reverend Beam's voice rang out, "be upon these vessels and all who come aboard, this day and forever. Amen."

"Amen," the crowd and captains said as one.

"Awoooooooo," the mayor agreed.

Grandpa grinned down at Nate and squeezed his shoulder. "Good Lord, let's eat."

As Nate and Gen licked the last of the syrup from their fingers, Councilman Lamprey announced the raffle drawing.

"Y'all gather around and get your tickets out. Somebody's going home with a brand-new truck today."

"Remember our agreement," he said to Gen.

She rolled her eyes.

"Chief Brandy," Councilman Lamprey said, "is a bit under the weather and can't be here to draw the winning ticket." The councilman turned to the old dog. "Mayor, would you kindly fetch someone to do the honors?"

The mayor wove his way through the crowd sniffing here and there until he came to Nate. "Rooo, rooo!"

The mayor grabbed Nate's wrist in his mouth and pulled him through the crowd. Hands reached out to touch him, along with hopeful whispers of "Pick mine, boy. Pick mine." By the time Nate got to the front of the crowd, his shirt was half hanging off, exposing the symphony of lightning-conducted scars.

The councilman held out a shoe box full of raffle tickets. "Stir them up real good, son."

Nate did.

"Now reach down and pick out the lucky ticket."

He swallowed hard and plunged his hand into the box. He held his breath as his fingers pulled out a ticket and handed it to the councilman.

The folks in the crowd were as quiet and still as they had been for the blessing.

"The winning ticket number is . . ." The councilman squinted at the ticket and adjusted his glasses. The crowd shifted impatiently.

"The winning number is 10299. Who has 10299?"

"Well I'll be dipped and fried," a voice from the back said. "It's my ticket." Grandpa held his ticket high. "I won a new truck!"

"That's not fair!"

"How come Jonah Harlow's having all the luck?"

Suspicious, resentful eyes darted from Nate to his grandpa and back.

"Come on up here, Jonah, and claim your prize," Councilman Lamprey called out in a bit-too-jovial voice.

Jonah Harlow made his way through the grumbling crowd. Only Chum Bailey's father patted him on the back and said, "Good for you, Jonah."

Councilman Lamprey thumped Grandpa on the back, then pumped his hand up and down. "Congratulations, Jonah! Here are the keys to your brand-new truck!" The councilman held them up for everyone to see. As he handed the keys over to Grandpa, he said, "Of course, none of us are going to know you, seeing as how you won't be driving old Alfred anymore."

Grandpa chuckled uneasily. A photographer from the newspaper snapped a picture or two. The crowd wandered away, still grumbling.

Nate walked with his grandpa over to their new truck, shining in the sun. It looked ready and raring to go.

"Sure is something, isn't it?" he said to his grandpa.

"Sure is." Grandpa kicked at a tire and gazed into the spotless bed of the truck. "Seems too nice to carry a bunch of bait buckets and dead fish around in."

Just then Reverend Beam, Mrs. Beam, and Gen walked up. "Whoowee, that is one fine truck, Jonah Harlow," the reverend said with a grin. "You think you'll be able to stand driving that thing?"

Grandpa smiled. "I don't know, but I'll sure give it a try." He ran one hand reverently along the flank of the truck. "Never owned anything brand-new before."

Two bouncing boys ran up to the truck and commenced to clamber up the sides. "Can we go for a ride?"

Grandpa grabbed the twins and pulled them off the truck. "Whoa now, boys. Let's not scuff up the shine."

Nate and Gen exchanged a look. Mrs. Beam took their hands and said, "Now, Leviticus and Joshua, you just calm down. Let's not mess around Mr. Harlow's nice new truck."

They all looked at the truck. Grandpa lifted his blue sombrero and scratched his head. "Sure is something," he said.

"Sure is," Levi agreed.

"Well, son," Grandpa said to Nate. "Let's take this puppy for a ride. You too, Gen."

Ricky and Connor trotted up. "Hey, Sparky, we're getting

up a baseball game over on the field. My dad's taking the winning team out for ice cream after," Ricky said.

"Yeah," Connor said. "We need you on our team so we'll win."

Nate swelled up with pride. He smiled up at his grandpa and puffed out his chest at Gen.

Reverend Beam smiled. "Didn't know you'd become such an athlete, Nate. Baseball's a fine game. The true American sport."

"Aw, he's not as good a player as me," Ricky said.

"Yeah," Connor said. "Mostly we need his luck."

Nate's heart sank, and his scrawny shoulders bunched up.

Gen pushed her glasses up the bridge of her nose and glared at the two boys. "May I remind you dunderheads that Nathaniel hit a home run the last time he played baseball in PE?"

"He did?" Grandpa asked in surprise.

"He did?" Joshua asked in awe.

"And," Gen said, as if she had witnessed the whole thing, which she surely had not, "he caught a fly ball in the outfield."

Nate looked at Gen like she'd grown two heads. How in the heck did she even know words like *fly ball* and *outfield*?

Ricky shrugged. "Well whatever, Sparky. You coming or not?"

He looked at the boys gathering over on the baseball field with longing. He looked up at his grandpa and then at Gen.

Gen took off her glasses and rubbed them with her shirttail, not looking at him. But oh, how she wanted to ride next to him in the new truck. And hadn't they made a bet? Why, after what happened, she'd even be willing to entertain the idea that he was right: The lightning had indeed changed something.

She cleared her throat. "Nathaniel, we had that bet, remember?"

Ricky snorted, Connor rolled his eyes. Nate's face burned.

Without looking at Gen or her family, he asked, "Can you pick me up later, Grandpa, in a couple of hours?"

And before anyone could answer, before he could see the stricken look on Gen's face, Nate raced off across the park to the baseball field with Ricky and Connor.

CHAPTER 13

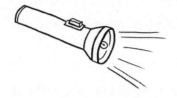

"Well would you look at that," Mrs. Beam said at the breakfast table Monday morning. She held up the front page of the *Paradise Beach Herald* for all the Beams to behold: DOES LIGHTNING BOY HAVE MIDAS TOUCH? Underneath the headline was a photograph of Nate and his grandpa smiling, holding aloft the keys to the new truck.

"Read it to us, Mama," Joshua said.

"Read it to us, *please*," Reverend Beam reminded his son.

Mrs. Beam cleared her throat. "Paradise Beach resident Nathaniel Harlow is fast becoming a bit of a local legend. Just two weeks ago, the young boy was struck by lightning while playing Goofy Golf on his birthday. Everyone, including the doctors at the Panama City Hospital, agreed it was nothing short of a miracle he survived, and now the lightning may have given our young resident the Midas touch. It seems Nate's Midas touch has helped his grandfather, Jonah Harlow, captain of the *Sweet Jodie*, win the brand-new Ford truck generously donated by Crystal Sands New and Used Cars."

Gen sighed and took her plate to the sink. "I'm going to school."

Reverend Beam followed his daughter down the narrow staircase from the living quarters to the church and out onto the front steps. He lifted his face to the sun and smiled. "Another day in paradise, daughter." He rested one large hand on her shoulder. "You going to do me proud at school today?"

Gen shrugged. Then she said, "Do you believe the lightning could have changed Nathaniel's luck?"

The reverend clasped his hands. "The Lord moves in mysterious ways, Gen."

"Yes sir, but could the *lightning* have taken his bad luck away and given him good luck?" she asked. "Not that I necessarily believe in luck, but let's just say, for the sake of argument —"

"Nothing to do with the lightning, daughter. The Lord giveth and the Lord taketh away." He bent and kissed his firstborn on the top of her head. "Best go catch the school bus now."

Gen planned what she would say to Nate about the raffle ticket as she trudged down the red clay road to the bus stop. Nate's abandonment of her for those boys still stung. On the other hand, she had made a promise to Nate. And a promise was a promise to keep.

"Nathaniel, while I still believe that luck — bad or good — is merely probability taken personally," she said aloud to the pines and the birds and shining sun, "I am beginning to consider the unlikely but fascinating idea that the lightning strike could have changed something in you. Still, we must not fall prey to . . ."

Gen stopped in her tracks. Nate was not waiting for her beneath the osprey nest topping the tall pine as he did every morning all school year. Except when he was struck by lightning.

She looked up the road one way and down the other. No Nate.

She wiped at the sweat beading her forehead and worried an eyebrow. A gray squirrel chattered from the branches of an oak.

"Cripes," she said.

The school bus eased to a stop and unfolded its doors. Gen looked up the road toward the Sweet Magnolia RV and Trailer Park. No Nate.

She climbed the steps of the school bus, her backpack bumping the back of her knees.

"Where's your partner in crime?" the bus driver asked.

"He's late," Gen said, squinting in the direction of the trailer park. "Perhaps we should wait for him, Mr. Tom."

The driver slammed the door shut and laughed. "I imagine his granddaddy's taking him to school today in that new truck with those fancy wheel rims. No need for him to ride this old can of sardines to school anymore."

She swallowed hard against the lump rising in her throat and headed for the back of the bus.

All day at school, she pondered the question of Nate's change of luck.

She pondered as she halfheartedly worked trigonometry problems on the whiteboard. She pondered while she pretended to read *The Tempest* by Shakespeare. She pondered while she put carts of books in Dewey Decimal order in the Paradise Beach branch of the Franklin County Library. And she pondered as she helped her mother with the dinner dishes.

"You're awful quiet tonight at dinner, sugar. Everything okay today at school?" Mrs. Beam asked.

"Yes ma'am," Gen said.

Mrs. Beam regarded her daughter out of the corner of her eye. "Did Nate bring good luck to that baseball team?"

She shrugged. "How should I know? I haven't seen or talked with him since then."

"Hmmm . . ." Mrs. Beam said as she dried the vegetable bowl. "That doesn't sound like Nate."

"He's been running around with his new friends, Ricky Sands and that bunch of philistines."

Mrs. Beam's eyes softened. She put her arm around Gen's shoulders and gave her a little squeeze. "Be patient with him, honey. It's such a new experience for someone like Nate to be popular, to be part of the in crowd."

"I wouldn't know," she said, leaning just for a fraction of a second into her mother's warm side.

"You know, Gen, it wouldn't hurt for you to make some friends besides Nate. There must be some other boys or girls at school who —"

She pulled away from her mother and shook her head. It had always just been her and Nate, which was all she needed.

"I'm going over to the dunes to watch for turtles," she said. "My charts indicate they should be here any day now."

Mrs. Beam smiled. "Why don't you take the girls with you? They've always wanted to go."

"Not this time, Mama. I'd need to train them first. It's not some game, you know."

Mrs. Beam sighed a weary sigh. "Okay, but you have to take them next time. Take a flashlight and don't be out too late."

Gen followed the path through the pines. The red clay dirt gave way to sand, and the pines bowed to dollarweed, scrubby brush, and honeysuckle vines. She climbed up and over a dune and dropped down to the beach — *her* beach.

At least that's the way she thought of it in her most private moments. Her heavy heart lifted and swelled like the tide and the moon. She closed her eyes and turned her most logical of minds over to the magic of the sea. She listened to the heave and sigh of the waves on the shore. She opened her nostrils wide and took in the perfume of salt and fish mixed together and served up on a warm, wet breeze. Sometimes, if she didn't know better, she would almost swear she could hear mermaids singing beneath the waves. She could *almost* believe in the magic the twins believed in to explain the sparkling phosphorescence in the water.

Gen straightened her glasses. What would Albert Einstein think of her imagining ridiculous things like mermaids and magic?

She picked her way along the shore, careful not to get her shoes wet. She could just hear Nate saying, *Come on, Gen, you got to take your shoes off and feel the sand and the Gulf!* Nate was a fish of a boy, that was for sure. He'd swim anywhere — off Henderson Pier, off the docks, way the heck out in the bay, under the waves in the Gulf — any time he took a mind to. She, on the other hand, couldn't swim a stroke.

She squared her shoulders and patrolled the shore for any infractions of the Turtle Rules. Save for one errant sand castle, folks were doing pretty well. She knocked the castle down and smoothed the sand.

As she proceeded along the beach, she watched for the telltale flipper tracks of turtles coming up to lay their eggs. "Hmm . . . not a single track." She took a notebook out of one of many pockets in her overalls and read back through her notes. "By my calculations, they should be coming up on shore to lay their eggs about now." Surely the turtles weren't becoming as unreliable as humans, were they? Could they? She gazed up at the sliver, fingernail of a moon. "They should have come with the full moon last week," she said, worrying an eyebrow.

Finally, at the far end of the beach, glowing white against the dark night stood the highest dune on Paradise Beach. How tall and unconquerable that dune had seemed to her and Nate when they first discovered it years ago. A towering mountain of a sand dune, a veritable Everest of sugar-white sand.

They had joined hands and dug their shoes and (Nate's) bare toes into the deep, cool sand, clambering up three steps, sliding back one, up three, down one, until they'd finally reached the top. They had stood atop the tallest dune on Paradise Beach taking in the vast wonder of the placid bay on one side and the restless Gulf of Mexico on the other, cradling their spit of land. It had forever after been their dune.

Gen scrambled up the dune and plopped down on the wind-scraped top. "I'm here," she said to no one in particular.

The only answer came from the wind rattling the sea oats and the *shhhhhh, shhhhhhhhh* of the waves upon the shore.

"Dang," she whispered. She felt a burn and a hot tickle in the back of her throat. "I will *not* cry," she declared through clenched teeth. "I *won't*."

She took a deep breath and began to sing. Now truth be told, Genesis Magnolia Beam could not carry a tune in a bucket. Even the good folks in her daddy's church choir politely discouraged her from joining their ranks. But out here on the dune, she and Nate sang. They sang church songs, popular songs from the radio, silly made-up songs. They sang loud above the wind and waves, they sang soft to the stars as they came out one by one. Nate even claimed the singing helped the turtles.

She closed her eyes, took a deep breath, and began to sing:

"This little light of mine, I'm gonna let it shine. This little light of mine . . ."

Her rusty bucket voice trailed off. Singing alone just wasn't the same.

She let out a sigh as watery and long as the turtles' journey to lay their eggs in the white sand. She dropped her head to her knees and sniffled. What had happened to *through thick and through thin*?

As the moon made its way across the sky and the turtles made their journey toward Paradise Beach, Gen cried.

CHAPTER 14

Later that week, Gen saw Chum Bailey sitting at a table in the school library, looking sad and forlorn as could be.

She didn't know much about the boy, just what she'd heard from Nate and what she'd observed: that he was picked on at least as much as she. She had some idea how he'd come by his nickname, Chum.

Gen sat across from the big boy and said, "Why so glum, Charles?"

Chum sighed. "Things ain't right, Genesis."

"Aren't," Gen corrected. "And explain, please."

Chum looked up from his hands and studied the girl. He had never actually talked with Genesis Beam. He had never dared to; she was too smart for the likes of him. Folks in town talked about how odd she was, so different from everyone else in Paradise Beach. Chum had always admired how clean and pressed her jeans were and how she stood up to people like Ricky Sands, but he'd never figured she'd talk to him.

"What's not right, Charles?" Gen asked again.

"Ever since my daddy got that money for winning the shrimp boat race, the other shrimpers are being mean to him," Chum said. "They say he didn't win the money fair and square."

Gen frowned. "How was his winning not fair?"

"Because Nate was on board. And seeing as how Nate has superpowers from the lightning and all, some are saying Daddy didn't deserve to win. No one wants to be friends with him anymore." The big boy hung his head. "I know how that feels, and it feels *terrible*, Genesis."

Gen studied the boy for a long moment. She had never noticed how kind his face was. In truth, she had never noticed him at all.

Maybe, she thought, her mother had been right about needing friends other than Nate.

"Could you help me look for turtle nests after school today?" she asked.

Chum looked up. "I thought Nate helped you with that."

She sighed. "He used to, until he got so busy with other

friends. It works better — the counting and watching, I mean — with two people."

"I don't think I'm as smart as Nate. I might be more of a bother than a help," he said, poking at the dirt beneath his fingernails with a paper clip. "Anyways, that's what my mama says."

"I beg to differ," Gen said.

Every day after school, Chum Bailey and Genesis Beam rode the bus back to Gen's house. They ate the snack prepared by Mrs. Beam and told her about their day at school, which was a study in contrasts.

Since Chum had started going to the beach with her, they had found turtle tracks, but no nests. Not a single one.

But they didn't give up.

"Hey, Gen," he called, waving something in the air. "Lookit what I found!" Chum trotted from the pile of sea-weed and driftwood he'd been pawing through and over to Gen. He held both hands out for her to see.

She gasped. "A flip-flop and a camera. Those have to be Nathaniel's!" And indeed they were. The flip-flop was a bit worse for wear, and the camera would most likely never work again. Still, Gen knew what they meant to Nate.

She took the camera from Chum and wiped away the wet sand. Maybe if she took it back to Nate, he would be her friend again and everything would be the way it was before. They would ride the bus together, monitor the turtles, and sit on their dune underneath the stars. Maybe with Chum too.

"Let's go find him," she said, grinning up at Chum.

"Do you know where he is?" he asked.

She nodded. "Where he always is." Slipping the camera and flip-flop into her beach bag, Gen trotted inland toward Billy Bowlegs Park.

She couldn't wait to see the look on Nate's face when he saw that she — not Ricky Sands or Connor or Buddy — *she* would reunite his missing shoes.

"Hey, who's that waving like a maniac over there?" Ricky Sands squinted across the baseball field, where a large someone waved from behind the chain-link fence.

The boys warming up for their after-school game stopped and looked toward the fence.

"Is that your big brother, Ricky?" Buddy asked.

Ricky shook his head. "Heck, I can't tell who it is."

Then a small someone stepped out from behind the big someone. It cupped its hands around its mouth. "Nathaniel! Nathaniel Harlow!" it called out.

Everyone looked at Nate. "Who's that?" Connor asked.

He shook his head and shrugged. "How should I know?" But he did. He'd know that voice anywhere. What the heck was Gen doing here? He tried his level best to shrink into his clothes so she wouldn't see him and would go away.

The two figures came trotting across the field, out into the sunlight, for God and all the boys to see.

"Oh. My. Heck," Ricky guffawed.

Buddy and Connor gaped and grinned. "I can't believe it. The two weirdest kids in the whole school."

"Hey, Nate," Chum said. "We been looking all over for you. It sure is lucky we looked here."

Nate purely did not feel lucky.

Ricky slapped Nate on the back. "Did you hear that, Sparky? They've been looking all over for you. You're the lucky one, as usual."

Gen studied the expression on Nate's face. She was not the best at reading people, she knew, but she had the distinct impression he was not happy to see them. That would all change, though, when she showed him the shoe and camera.

She elbowed Chum out of the way and smiled at Nate. "I brought you something."

The boys hooted and hollered. "Ooo, Sparky, your girlfriend brought you something!" Ricky made smoochie noises.

Nate's face burned with humiliation.

Gen ignored the boys. She pulled a bag from behind her back and handed it to Nate.

"Open it," she said. Both she and Chum were grinning, Nate decided, like a couple of idiots.

The boys crowded around him. "Oh, I can't wait to see what Sparky's girlfriend brought him, can you?" Connor said in a high, girly voice.

Nate glared at Gen and Chum. Why did they have to show up here and ruin everything?

"Come on and see what it is," Chum implored.

"Yeah," Ricky said. "Let's see." He grabbed the bag from Nate and pulled out the battered flip-flop.

Nate gasped. His shoe!

Gen grinned. The look on his face was exactly what she'd expected. "We found your camera too. It's in the bag," she said.

Connor grabbed the camera out of the bag and held it up for all to see. Water streamed from the case. Buddy grabbed the camera and doubled over with laughter. "What a great gift. A broken camera!"

Part of Nate wanted to grab the flip-flop from Ricky and the camera from Buddy and dance with joy; another part, though, wanted Gen and Chum and the shoe and camera to just disappear. Now.

Gen tried to grab the camera from Buddy. "That's Nathaniel's, not yours. Give it back to him!" Buddy shoved her away, knocking her to the ground.

"Hey!" Chum cried. "Leave her alone!" He pulled Gen to her feet. She looked from Buddy to Nate. Surely he would stand up for her like he always had before. He would tell those boys a thing or two.

Gen picked up the flip-flop and camera from the weeds. Someone must have stepped on it in the scuffle, because the case was cracked.

"Here," she said, handing it to Nate with a shaking hand.

"Oh yes, Sparky," Buddy said, sneering. "Take your camera and shoe and go play with your girlfriend and the big dummy."

Gen felt Chum take a step back. She waited for Nate to tell the boys they could all go take a flying leap to the moon.

Instead, he pushed the flip-flop and waterlogged camera away, none too gently. They fell to the ground. "What do I want with just one flip-flop and a broken camera?" he said.

Gen's plucked-over eyebrows bunched up in confusion. "But now you can bring the shoes back together, like you always wanted."

Buddy and Connor about fell to the ground laughing. Ricky frowned.

Nate felt words building up inside him like molten lava in a volcano. He knew they were terrible words, *hurtful* words, *mean* words, but he couldn't stop himself.

"You are *so weird*, Gen. You're as weird as your name."

Her eyes widened and her mouth dropped open. "I don't get it. . . ."

"You *never* do," he said.

Gen pulled frantically at her eyebrows. She felt a huge burning knot rising up from her stomach all the way to her eyes. "What is wrong with you?" she whispered.

Nate grabbed his baseball glove. "There's nothing wrong with me. *You're* the weirdo."

And before he could see the expression on her face, he turned his back on her. "Come on," he said to the boys. "Let's go play ball. I'm feeling lucky."

Gen watched Nate strut across the weedy field. Her legs shook. Her hands shook. Her insides shook.

Chum patted her on the shoulder. "I'm sorry he said those things to you. I'm used to it, but . . ."

Gen tried to say something, something logical that would explain Nate's behavior. No words came. All she could feel was a deep, deep hurt like she'd never felt before. All she could hear were his words cutting into her like a knife: *You're the weirdo.*

She pulled away from Chum and ran faster than she ever had, away from Nate and the terrible, awful words.

CHAPTER 15

The smartest girl in Franklin County (and maybe all of Florida) sat atop the roof of The Church of the One True Redeemer and Everlasting Light, arms hugging her knees to her chest and eyes dripping with tears.

When her mama told her for the third time to come down for supper, she said, "I can't, Mama. I have to think."

When her little brothers tried to clamber out onto the roof to join her, she said, "Go back in. I need to think."

When her little sisters poked their heads out the window and asked, "Are you crying?" Gen shouted, "Go away, I'm thinking."

And later, her daddy, who was purely terrified of heights, scooted oh-so-carefully out onto the roof, touched her face, and said, "Daughter, would you like me to sit here with you?"

She sniffled and shook her head. "Thanks, though, Daddy."

Reverend Beam scooted oh-so-carefully back across the roof and through the window. "Don't stay out there much longer, honey," he said. "You're worrying your mama."

Gen hugged her knees closer and let her gaze drop to her homemade weather station. She'd won the second grade science fair with this project. Her father said it was a heck of a lot more reliable than that weatherman on the TV who didn't know a barometer from an anemometer.

Measuring air pressure and wind speed made sense to Gen. Everyone said the weather was a fickle thing, but she always said, "There's nothing fickle about it; you just have to know how to measure it. It's science, not a 'thing.'"

What *didn't* make sense to the smartest girl in Franklin County (and probably all of Florida) was Nate. Nate and his hurtful words. He'd always stood up for her, and she for him. Her mother said they were like peanut butter and jelly; Nate's grandpa said they were like a rod and reel. They fit, like a turtle and its shell. They were better together. Who wanted just a plain ol' peanut butter sandwich? And how would a rod work without a reel? It wasn't logical.

But as illogical as it seemed, something in Nate *had* changed with the lightning strike. Even she had to admit it. He had, in fact, for whatever reason, become very lucky. Everything he wanted, he got. Everything he touched turned to gold, so to speak.

Gen shook her head and wiped her sleeve across her drippy nose. Even if that were true, why would it have to change being best friends? From the first time she'd spotted that small boy, shoulders hunched against the stares and taunts of the kids on the school bus, she'd understood him. She'd glared at the same kids who wouldn't sit with her on the bus because she was "weird" and gone straight to the back and sat down next to him. They'd sat together every day (880 days, she quickly calculated) since.

She'd argued with her science teacher the other day about whether or not Einstein's theory of relativity opened the possibility for time travel. Her teacher said it was the stuff of bad science fiction novels. Gen had quoted Einstein as saying, "The separation between past, present, and future is only an illusion." Her teacher had suggested (rather sarcastically, now that she thought about it) that if she knew so much, maybe she should build a time machine for next year's science project and take a trip.

Gen sighed. If she *could* build a time machine, the first thing she'd do is go back to Nate's birthday — before Goofy Golf, before the lightning had struck the golf club, when everything was the way it had always been. Because what would a turtle be without its shell?

CHAPTER 16

Nate stood beside Ricky, Connor, and Buddy, gazing at the two-foot-tall glass jar full of jelly beans on the counter at Jean's Drugstore. A sign taped to the jar read GUESS THE EXACT NUMBER OF JELLY BEANS AND WIN FREE ICE CREAM FLOATS FOR A MONTH!

"Wow, ice cream floats for a month," Ricky said. "I could eat five a day."

"Shoot, that's nothing," Buddy said. "I bet I could eat ten a day."

Nate sighed. Ice cream floats reminded him of hot summer afternoons eating Mrs. Beam's ice cream floats on the Beam family's back porch, which reminded Nate of Gen. And that reminded him with a sick feeling in his belly of the words he'd said to her two days before.

"How many thousands of jelly beans do you think could be in there?" Connor said, squinting at one side of the jar, then the other.

Buddy rubbed his hands together like a greedy squirrel. "Doesn't matter," he said. He gave Nate a poke. "We've got our secret weapon here. Whatever he guesses will win us the floats, right, Sparky?"

He shrugged uneasily. "I'm not sure how that would work."

"Isn't that like cheating?" Ricky Sands pointed out.

Buddy grabbed Nate's wrist and shoved his hand against the jar. "No it's not. Tell us what it says."

"I don't know." Nate tried his best to squirm his way out of Buddy's grip.

Jean Robbs, owner of the drugstore, appeared behind the counter and glared down at the boys. She pointed at Nate and said, "His guess doesn't count." And then she narrowed her eyes and said, "And any guess you boys give doesn't count either."

"That's not fair!" Connor protested.

Jean Robbs planted her fists on her hips and said, "Like

your friend there said, it'd be cheating. Now get on out of my drugstore."

The boys slunk out into the afternoon heat.

"Nuts," Buddy said.

"I told you," Ricky said.

"Shut up, Ricky," Connor said. Then he pointed at Nate. "You ruined it."

This set the boys to arguing like nobody's business. Ricky said he always knew it was cheating, and Buddy said since when did Ricky become such a goody-two-shoes, and Connor said if Buddy hadn't been so loud in the drugstore, the owner would have never suspected what they were doing anyway.

"Cheater!"

"Goody-two-shoes!"

"Loudmouth!"

The boys shouted at one another as they stalked off in three different directions, leaving Nate all by himself on the hot sidewalk.

"Jeez Louise," he muttered.

As he started toward the docks to see if he could find his grandpa, two little girls dressed in identical pink shorts and purple shirts came toward him. He smiled and waved. "Hey, Ruth. Hey, Rebecca." He hadn't realized until he saw them coming up the street how much he missed the Beam family.

The two girls raced up to him. But instead of their usual squealing and jumping and climbing, they stopped in front of Nate, glared their hardest, meanest glares, reared back, and kicked him in the shins.

Nate doubled over in pain. "Ow! Ow! What the heck was that for?"

"You made our sister cry, that's what," Ruth spat.

"Yeah," Rebecca said. "You're just like all the other mean kids," and she gave Nate another swift kick in the shin for good measure before they stalked off, arm in arm, into the drugstore.

He sat down on the curb, rubbing his shins. He didn't know which hurt worse, though, his shins or the fact that he'd made Gen cry. Surely Rebecca and Ruth were wrong. In all the years he'd known Genesis Beam, he'd never, ever seen her cry. No matter what the mean kids at school called her or what they said about her, she acted like it didn't bother her at all. Heck, he always figured Gen had a tough shell, just like the loggerhead turtles she cared so much about.

Two rain-soaked nights later, Grandpa and Nate sat slumped in their little silver trailer staring at their broken television.

"I reckon the shrimpers and the charter boat crews are coming in about now," Grandpa said with a sigh. "They'll be washing down their boat decks and heading on over to the Laughing Gull Grill, hashing over the latest scuttlebutt."

Nate turned and asked, "Why aren't you going over to the Laughing Gull?"

"They think I'm somehow cheating, getting all the good charter trips. And of course, winning that truck didn't help," he said.

"Because of me," Nate said.

Grandpa gave him a little shake. "No, son, just funny notions people get in their heads. And just between you and me, I'm not sure how much I like that new truck, anyway," Grandpa confessed. "I feel guilty every time I put a bait bucket or my old crab traps in the back and get into the front in dirty clothes. It's almost like the truck takes it personally. Does that sound crazy?" Grandpa asked.

"No sir, not to me," Nate said.

"Why aren't you out with those new friends of yours?" Grandpa asked.

Nate rubbed his thumb over the letter *L* burned into the palm of his hand. "They all just fight over me now. They think I can bring them good luck and that I have some kind of Midas touch. They don't really care about me," he said.

Grandpa put his arm around Nate's shoulder and drew him close. "Like I said, folks get funny notions in their heads." He took Nate's scarred hand and stared into the palm. Lightly he traced his finger over the *L* and the *Y*. "Do you think something did happen?"

Nate nodded. "Yes sir. I think even Gen might believe it now, and you know how she is."

"Your grandmother used to say 'There are more things in heaven and earth than are dreamt of.' It's from Shakespeare, I think."

"Gen would know," Nate said.

Grandpa nodded. "That she would. Speaking of Gen," Grandpa continued, "seems you two aren't spending much time together anymore."

Nate shrugged. "She doesn't exactly fit in with Ricky and Connor and Buddy. She doesn't like to do the same stuff."

Grandpa stood and stretched his arms over his head. "Having new friends is always nice, but don't forget your old ones. They're the ones that'll stick by you through thick and thin."

Nate felt like someone had punched him in the stomach, hearing those familiar words.

"Yes sir," he mumbled as his grandpa headed outside.

Nate wandered back to his bedroom. He flung himself upon his bed, his eyes wandering around the tiny room: the faded curtains, the bookcase made of cinder blocks and plastic milk crates. His wandering gaze came to rest upon the one red high-top tennis shoe in his closet. Oh, how he missed wearing those old sneakers, how they seemed to know every nook and cranny of his feet. He'd never been able to bring himself to go back to Goofy Golf to look for the other shoe. He sighed and looked away.

"Sometimes I wish it'd never happened," he said to the photograph of his parents. "I wish it could be taken back."

But how to undo the luck the lightning had given him? Nate wondered as he listened to the rain drum against the trailer windows. He could only think of one person in all of Franklin County who might know.

CHAPTER 17

Chum Bailey sat by himself on Mr. Tom's school bus, thinking about friendship. It made him sad that the only friends he had in the world, Nate and Gen, were not friends with each other anymore. It seemed to Chum, whose best friend had always been Mr. Bowditch the cat, that if you were lucky enough to have a friend, you were lucky enough. If you had more than one friend, why, you were just about the luckiest son of a pirate there was. You didn't call them names and you didn't throw them over for new friends; you stuck by them even when you were mad. The night before, he'd wished on the first star that Nate and Gen would work things out and they could all be friends.

The bus doors closed. Someone slid into the seat beside Chum and whispered, "Where's Gen?"

Chum gaped at the apparition sitting low in the seat beside him: a sweatshirt three sizes too big, hood pulled over the face, dark sunglasses, and gloves. But what really threw him for a loop was the badly scribbled mustache on its upper lip.

"Who the heck are you?" Chum asked.

The vision slunk lower down into the seat. "Shhh, not so loud. It's me, Nate."

"Nate?" the big boy asked in disbelief. "What in blue blazes —"

"Shhhhh!" Nate hissed. "I'm in disguise."

Chum frowned. "But it's not Halloween."

Nate looked from one side of the bus to the other. "I know that. I changed clothes after school. I don't want anyone on the bus to recognize me."

"I thought you liked everybody recognizing you, being so popular now and all."

"I was, but it's gotten too crazy. Folks are fighting *over* me and *because* of me."

The two boys contemplated this fact as the bus bumped along the sandy road.

"Why are you riding the bus?" Nate asked.

"I'm going over to Gen's house to check in on her," Chum replied. "Friends do that," he added.

"Is she still mad at me?"

Chum frowned. "You hurt her bad, Nate. That's why she hasn't been coming to school, and you know how Gen feels about school."

Nate's heart sunk low as a crab's belly. He surely did know how much Gen loved school. She had to be the only kid in Paradise Beach and probably in all of Florida who dreaded summer vacation.

The bus rolled to a stop beside the tall pine tree. Chum grabbed his plastic grocery bag full of books for Gen and stood.

Nate slunk out of the bus behind the big boy. At the bottom of the steps, Mr. Tom called out, "Lookin' good, Nate." Nate sighed. Chum had blown his cover.

The sun beat down hot as blazes as they walked up the red clay road, through the pines, to The Church of the One True Redeemer and Everlasting Light. Sweat trickled down Nate's back and plastered his hair to his head underneath the sweatshirt hood. He wiped at the sweat on his upper lip. His hand came back smeared with mustache.

"I need to ask Gen about something. Do you think she'll talk to me?" he asked.

Chum studied a crow up in a tree. "Hard to say. What is it you need to talk with her about?"

"I got to find out how to get rid of this good luck. I figure she's about the only person smart enough to know how to do that."

"You want to be *un*lucky again? Why would you?"

"Well, I don't know that I want to be unlucky again," he tried to explain. "Not if I can help it. But I want things to be more like the way they were before I got struck by lightning."

Chum shook his head. His mama always said folks were never satisfied with what the good Lord gave them, and that certainly seemed to be the case with Nate.

He shrugged. "I reckon we'll see when we get there."

The two boys stood in the shadows of the pine forest, gazing across the oyster shell parking lot of The Church of the One True Redeemer and Everlasting Light. As always, the doors to the church stood wide open to the sun and the salt air and anyone who happened to wander by. Nate heard the flutelike voices of Ruth and Rebecca drifting from the sanctuary. He ached to see them, but his shins still smarted from the kicking they'd given him a few days before.

"Maybe you should go in and talk with her first," he said, running his hand along a bumpy shinbone.

He watched from the shadows of the trees as Chum ambled across the parking lot. He heard the laughing, singing, squabbling, tripping voices of the girls call out, "Charles! It's Charles!" and watched them fling their arms around Chum's waist and attempt the long climb up to his arms. Nate's throat knotted and burned as boy and twins disappeared into the dark coolness of the church.

"Where's your sister?" Chum asked the twins as they investigated the pockets on his shirt where he was known to keep lemon drops.

"She's up on the roof," Ruthie said. "She won't come down for nothing."

"She's making Mama worried," said Rebecca.

The girls swung around Chum's neck and rode him piggyback up the stairs to the living quarters.

"She *says* she's busy thinking," Ruthie added.

Chum poked his head into the kitchen, where Mrs. Beam

was just pulling a tray of something wonderful-smelling out of the oven. Her face broke open with relief at the sight of the boy.

"Oh, Charles, I'm glad you're here. Maybe you can get Gen to come in off that roof and eat something."

Chum remembered once when Mr. Bowditch got himself up a tree because of some dog and wouldn't come down for hours and hours. He had climbed up the tree in the middle of a hurricane (well, it had seemed almost as bad as a hurricane), branches swinging every which way and rain about to drown him, and lured Mr. Bowditch down with a snickerdoodle and a bowl of sweet milk.

"May I have some milk and cookies, please?" he asked.

Mrs. Beam blinked. "Well, of course, Charles, but what about Gen?"

He took the still-warm cookies and the glass of milk. "I reckon if it worked on a cat, it'll work on Gen," he said, and headed for the open window.

Chum eased out the window and onto the roof. There sat Gen, perched like a crow beside her weather station, peering through a pair of binoculars.

"Hey," he called.

She didn't even turn to look at him.

He edged over closer. "I brought you some cookies and milk," he said. "The cookies are still warm from the oven. They're chocolate chip and oatmeal — your favorite." Chum's stomach rumbled in reminder that they were, in fact, his favorite too.

Gen lowered the binoculars and fixed him with a look. "Why did you bring Nathaniel here?"

Chum swallowed hard and inched a little closer. He remembered how Mr. Bowditch had hissed at him up in the tree. He put on his best cat-soothing voice and replied, "Nate needs your help, Gen. He says you're likely the only one smart enough to help him."

"Humph," she snorted. She raised the binoculars back to her eyes. "What the heck's he doing all bundled up in a stupid hooded sweatshirt when it's" — Gen lowered the binoculars and squinted at her weather station — "eighty-nine degrees with a relative humidity of sixty-three percent?"

"He's in disguise because everybody's fighting over him," he relayed, although it really didn't make a whole heck of a lot of sense to him.

"I wouldn't know how that is," Gen mumbled. She scooted over next to Chum and took a cookie and the glass of milk.

Chum smiled. Just like Mr. Bowditch.

"Anyways," he said, "Nate really wants things to go back more the way they were before he got struck by lightning and he got lucky and popular and all. He says you're probably the only one who would know how to make that work."

Gen frowned. "How should I know?" She moved away from Chum, but not before he caught the teary glint in her eye and the stubborn set to her chin. "Besides, give me one good reason I should help him after the things he said to me." Her chin quivered.

Chum sighed. "Because, Gen, up until a little while ago, he was your best friend in the world."

He waited in the hot sun on top of the roof for her reply. None came. He left the plate of cookies and headed carefully back toward the window with the glass of milk. Just as he was half in the window, Gen called out, "If he really believes everything changed because of the lightning strike, then it's only logical he'd have to get struck again for it to change back."

Chum frowned. "Okay, Gen. I'll tell him."

The big boy took the glass of milk back to the kitchen. Mrs. Beam looked at him and said, "So? Did she come in?"

Chum shook his head. "People are a lot more complicated than cats."

"She said *what*?" Nate asked for the third time.

Chum pushed the hood off of Nate's head so he could hear better. "I *said* she's still mad at you!" he hollered. "And she said if you want your luck to change back, you'd probably have to get struck by lightning again!"

Nate shook his head and gazed up at the figure sitting on top of the church. "I heard you the first time, Chum, but how the heck do I get struck by lightning again?" Not to mention that even if he could, who's to say it wouldn't kill him this time? "It's not like I planned it the last time."

Chum and Nate took the shortcut through the woods over to the Sweet Magnolia RV and Trailer Park. Dark clouds scudded across the sky, covering the sun. Thunder rumbled in the distance.

"Well, there was that Benjamin Franklin feller, with his kite and key. We studied him in science class this year," Chum said.

Nate shivered despite the sweatshirt, and his head pounded. "I remember that too," he said, eyeing the sky nervously. "But I don't have a kite."

Thunder cracked, closer this time. Lightning flashed so close, the hair stood up on his arms and neck. As if they had a mind of their own, his legs and feet sprinted as fast as they could go to the trailer.

"Hang on, Nate! Wait up!"

Nate threw himself into the trailer and sprinted down the hallway as lightning lit the sky and rain came down in sheets. Chum came in behind him, shaking water off like a wet dog.

"Whoowee! That's a real gully washer, ain't it?"

Nate was nowhere in sight. "Nate?" Chum called.

In the back of the trailer, Chum heard a tiny, muffled moan.

"Nate?" Chum whispered as he followed the sound to the back bedroom. The lumpy covers on the bed shook with fright. Thunder boomed. The covers moaned.

Chum sat down on the bed and patted the trembling mound. "It's okay, Nate. It's okay."

CHAPTER 18

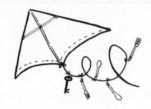

When Nate woke the next morning, he heard his grandpa cussing up a storm in the kitchen.

He slipped the lucky rabbit's foot into his pocket, said good morning to his parents, and glanced at the box full of single-shoe photographs.

He followed the scent of burnt toast from his bedroom to the kitchen and watched as his grandpa banged his fist on the toaster. "You useless hunk of junk, you sorry excuse for an appliance!" He jerked the plug out of the wall. "I should just toss you in the bay and be rid of you."

"Grandpa," he said, "why are you here? I thought you had a full day of charters." Nate couldn't remember a Saturday morning, or any morning for that matter, since everything had turned lucky that his grandpa had been home. He had to admit it was kind of nice.

All the bluster went out of his grandpa's sails. He slumped onto the couch. "Boat's not running," he mumbled.

Nate eased over to the toaster, plugged it back in, and set two slices of bread to toast.

"Why not?" he asked. Grandpa always said the *Sweet Jodie* was as steady as a July day.

Through clenched teeth, Grandpa replied, "Someone sabotaged it."

Ding! Two perfect pieces of toast popped out of the toaster and landed side by side on the plate. The toaster sighed with happy contentment.

Nate smeared the toast with butter and jam and took them over to his grandpa. "Why in the world would somebody hurt the *Sweet Jodie*?"

Grandpa looked at the toast — truly wondrous in its perfection — then at the toaster, and shook his head. "They're trying to hurt me. The other captains have been grumbling for the last few weeks that I'm getting all the business and taking money away from them. I reckon someone figured the best way to fix that was to kill my boat."

Nate's mouth went dry. "I'm sorry, Grandpa. It's all my fault."

Grandpa patted the miserable boy's shoulder. "Now, Nate, it's not your fault. It's . . . well, it's just too much of a good thing, I reckon. When folks think you're taking something away that belongs to them, it brings out the worst in them."

Nate chewed the side of his thumb as he pondered this point. Seemed to him his good luck was bringing out just about the worst in everybody.

"I bet I can fix it, Grandpa," he said, brightening. "I think I might've fixed Mr. Bailey's boat during the race, and it was just about dead as a doornail."

Grandpa sighed. "They took parts out. That's not something anybody can fix. I'm going to have to ride all the way over to Panama City to buy new ones. And who's to say, even once I do that, they won't steal them again?"

Nate was thunderstruck. He never in a million trillion years would have thought someone in Paradise Beach would *steal*! Not in his little town. Fishing folks always helped each other. The idea of it made him sick through and through. This had to stop, and he was the only one who could make things the way they used to be.

Grandpa pushed himself off the couch. "Well, there's nothing for it but to spunk up and do it. Want to go over to Panama City with me?"

"Yes sir," he said. "And while we're there, could I buy a kite?"

⚡

Late that afternoon, Chum Bailey held the kite aloft, the sun shining through the orange-and-black paper wings. He let out a low whistle. "This is one fine kite," he said. "It sure enough looks like a monarch butterfly, don't it?"

Nate thought about the hundreds and hundreds of monarchs they'd see in the fall, all flying along their zigzaggity, invisible trail to Mexico for the winter. When Gen told him butterflies could fly that far, he said he'd never heard of anything so miraculous. "It's not a miracle," Gen had said. "It's science." But even she didn't sound too convinced of that fact.

"We still need a key, though," Nate pointed out. "A big one."

"I bet my daddy's got one in that old shed of his back behind our house. He's got practically everything in there and then some," Chum said with pride. Then he frowned.

"But Nate, how in the world are you going to do this? We can get all the kites and keys in the world, but if you can't stand to be out in a storm, it's not going to work."

"I got to. It's not just about me anymore. Let's go find a key," Nate said. "And then I need a favor from you."

"What's that?"

"Our TV's broke and Grandpa left the radio on his boat," he said, as if this was a new occurrence, which it surely was not. "I need you to watch the news to see when the next storm is. We'll meet down on the beach by the old pier."

Two days later at school, Chum tapped Nate on the shoulder during Mr. Peck's explanation about the difference between a metaphor and a simile.

"The weatherman says there's a big thunderstorm coming in tonight," Chum whispered too loudly.

"Mr. Bailey, is there something you care to share with the class?" Mr. Peck asked in a withering voice.

Chum shrugged. "Sure." He stood and looked around at the room full of smirking, eye-rolling faces. "There's a storm coming in tonight. The weatherman over in Panama City says so."

The tiny blue vein in Mr. Peck's temple bulged and throbbed. He looked up at the ceiling and muttered, "Only twenty-two more days, Peck, only twenty-two more days . . ."

Nate buried his nose in his grammar book, trying not to laugh.

⚡

As storms go on the Gulf of Mexico, it was a puny one. Lightning sputtered lethargically across the sky, thunder muttered disinterestedly, and the wind could hardly be bothered to gust above twenty-five miles an hour.

Chum scanned the dunes for Nate. He was beginning to wonder if his friend had chickened out. He sighed. He couldn't blame him after what he'd been through.

A small figure crept and crabbed its way over the dunes and down toward the beach, the kite clutched to his chest. Every time lightning flashed, a long, low moan issued forth from the figure.

Chum waved his arm. "Over here, Nate!" He ran across the beach to the pathetic figure cowering in a clump of dollarweed. "I'm sorry," he said as he reached down for his friend. "It's the only way back to how it used to be."

Nate stood on quivering knees and eyed the sky. "I know."

Chum pried the kite away from Nate's chest. "Just hold on to it like this while I tie the key and stuff on the string." He tied the rusty metal key they'd found in his daddy's shed onto the kite string along with a bunch of old silverware they'd found in a moldy box.

Nate looked doubtfully at all the metal hanging from the kite's tail. "I don't think it's going to fly with all that weight, Chum."

"Sure it will," he said. "Just try."

Nate took a deep breath to swallow down the bile rising in his throat. He set off running along the shore, the wet sand sucking at his bare feet and needles of rain stinging his eyes. His head pounded and his lightning scars burned like fire.

A particularly frisky gust of wind took notice of the boy. It slipped under the belly of the kite and pushed it skyward. Nate ran faster and faster, letting out string as he went.

"Run, Nate, run!" Chum called. He looked to the skies and prayed, "Please, just strike him a little bit. Just enough for his own good."

The kite rose higher and higher. Lightning lit the spoons and forks and the old metal key. It crackled above Nate's head and then danced off to the side.

His stomach heaved. His legs seemed to have a mind of their own. "Please, please," he prayed. "Please don't kill me."

Wind is a fickle thing. It is not something you can set store by. This particular wind playing with kite and boy was easily distracted, even for wind. It soon tired. With one final push, it slipped from beneath the kite and set out across the dunes, like a hound dog on a fresh scent, for Mr. Wood's wind chimes.

The kite plummeted to the ground. Nate dropped to his knees and heaved his supper into the sand.

"I'm sorry, Nate," Chum said. "I don't think Mr. Franklin's experiment is going to work. I guess it was a dumb idea."

"That's okay," Nate said. He looked up at the egg-shaped moon peeking out from behind the clouds. "Looks like the storm has passed anyway."

At the word *storm*, a shudder ran through his body.

"Let's head back to my house," Chum said, helping his friend to his feet. "My daddy will make you a cup of his special seasick tea, okay?"

Gen watched the two boys trudge up and over the rain-swept dunes from her rooftop perch. Slowly, she lowered her binoculars. She shook her head in wonder and disbelief. "Holy Einstein. I can't believe they tried it. They actually tried it."

CHAPTER 19

Genesis Beam made herself a liverwurst on rye sandwich, wrapped it carefully in wax paper (so the sandwich would not get any pickle juice on it from her dill pickle spear), and tucked it into her Albert Einstein backpack.

"Where you off to, sugar?" Mrs. Beam asked.

"Down to the beach to look for turtle tracks and nests. There's something strange going on with the turtles this year, and I need to figure it out." She'd wrestled with this puzzle all day at school, causing her, for the first time in her life, to miss a question on a quiz.

Mrs. Beam listened to the wind rattle the windows. "I have to take the boys to their swimming lessons, so you'll need to take the girls with you."

Gen frowned. "This is serious business. The turtles are not only not laying eggs, they've stopped digging nests."

Mrs. Beam slapped two peanut butter and banana sandwiches together and stuffed towels in a bag. "Well then, your sisters can help you figure it out."

"But Mama —"

"You know Ruthie loves a challenge, and Rebecca never misses the tiniest detail," Mrs. Beam continued.

Gen's bottom lip stuck out like the high dive at the public swimming pool. "I'll take them next time."

Mrs. Beam froze. Slowly she turned around and faced her daughter. "I do not believe I *asked* you to take them with you, did I?"

"But Mama . . ."

Mrs. Beam was not one to yell or holler when she was angry. No, her voice got lower, quieter, and calm as ice. "Genesis Magnolia Beam, I ask precious little of you."

Gen gulped and looked down at her shoes. When her mama used her middle name along with the rest of her name, she knew she was in a boatload of trouble.

"All I'm asking of you is to take your little sisters, who, in case you hadn't noticed, purely worship the ground you walk on, over to the beach with you to look for turtle nests. I'm not asking you *not* to go to the beach; I'm not asking you to play little girl games with them. Right?"

"Yes ma'am," Gen whispered, not looking up.

Gently Mrs. Beam took her daughter's chin in her hand and tipped her face up. She looked into her firstborn's unfathomable eyes. "You need to bring your head out of that shell of yours and take a look at the world around you, the *people* around you," she said. "You just might be surprised by what you see."

Gen swallowed down the lump lodged in her throat. "Yes, Mama," she said.

"Now," Gen said, pointing her pencil at the two grinning, hopping-foot-to-foot, pulling-off-their-shoes-as-quick-as-they-could twin girls. "This is a serious job you're here to help me with. It takes a keen eye for detail and —"

"Look out there!" Ruthie cried, hopping up and down, pointing out to sea. "Porpoises! A whole bunch of them!"

Gen sighed. "Yes, Ruth, I saw them. But we're not here to look for porpoises, we're here to look for —"

Rebecca gasped as a flight of cormorants sliced through the wind, throwing sharp shadows on the shore. "Oh my!"

And being Rebecca, she threw her head back and burst into a spasm of poetry: "I think that I shall never see a poem as lovely as cormorants at sea."

The two girls followed after their big sister like happy little ducklings, exclaiming over all wonders, great and small.

"Lookit! I found a whole sand dollar!"

"Did you see that pelican dive in headfirst?"

"Oh, I just *love* sandpipers, don't you?"

"Look, Gen, I found a devil's purse." Ruth held the black pouch up by one of its four curved horns for her big sister to see. "Why would the devil have a purse if he's a boy, huh, Gen?"

Gen didn't know whether to laugh or cry. She shook her head and said, "It's just the egg sack of a skate, Ruth. It's not really the devil's purse. That's just a made-up name." Both girls frowned up at their big sister. "Made up for fun," Gen explained. "A skate is kind of like a stingray, only smaller, although technically it's a relative of the shark."

"That's weird," Ruth said, turning the small, hard pouch over in her hands.

"I think it's amazing," Rebecca announced.

Gen thought it really was somewhere in between the two. "Weirdly amazing," she summed up. "Now, let's look for turtle signs."

All three girls studied the sand as they walked along the beach. Gen had to admit, once the twins put their minds to it, they were pretty darned good at spotting loggerhead tracks. By the time they reached her and Nate's dune, they had counted eight sets of tracks. But no nests.

"Holy moly, look at that!" both girls cried at once. "It's the biggest sand dune in the whole world!"

A prickle of pride plucked at the corners of Gen's mouth. "Well, probably not in the whole *world*, but it is the biggest — as far as I know — on Paradise Beach. You can see a long ways from up there."

The girls looked up at their big sister with awe. "You've been up to the top?" Rebecca asked, eyes wide.

Gen shrugged and did her best to suppress a grin. "Sure, all the time." She and Nate, that is.

Before you could say The Church of the One True

Redeemer and Everlasting Light, the twins tossed their shoes and beach-found treasures onto the sand and did their level best to race each other to the top.

"Wait!" Gen cried. "Wait for me!"

And before she realized what she was about to do, she yanked her shoes off, dug her toes into the cool, sugar-white sand, and made her way up the flank of the dune. "I must admit," she said as she arrived panting at the top, "it's a lot easier to climb the dune with one's shoes off." She smiled at her little sisters. "Now, let me orient you to our surroundings by —"

Ruthie could have given a flip about orienting. She flung herself onto her side and commenced to roll down the dune at an alarming speed. "Wheeeeeeeeeeee!" Which was promptly followed by an equally enthusiastic, identical roll and "Wheeeeeeeeeeee!"

Up the dune, down the dune, up the dune, down the dune the girls went with boundless energy, until they looked like laughing, stumbling, giggling, sugar-coated gingerbread cookies.

"Are you done now?" Gen asked, wiggling her bare toes in the salty air.

"Yes," Ruth said.

"No," Rebecca said.

"Just one more roll," Gen said. Rebecca flung herself one last time down the dune while Gen did her best to brush sand from every square inch of Ruth. "Mama's going to skin us alive when she sees what a mess you are."

"Hey, Gen," Rebecca called. "Come see what I found."

She rolled her eyes. "What now?"

She and Rebecca plunge-stepped their way down the dune to where Ruthie crouched over something.

"Rebecca, we really need to go. Mama's going to be —"

The little girl moved aside and pointed. "It's a turtle nest, isn't it?"

Gen gasped and dropped to her knees. Before her was a telltale sand mound with tracks leading to and from. Gently, oh-so-gently, she scraped away the sand heap. There, nestled like a bunch of left-behind Ping-Pong balls, was a clutch of eggs.

Praise the Lord and pass the peas! The first nest of the season, and her sister had found it! Gen did a very un-Gen-like thing: She let out a whoop, picked Rebecca up, and twirled her around. "You found it, Rebecca! You found a nest! Wait until I tell Nathaniel!"

But would he even care?

CHAPTER 20

"I just don't get it," Gen said as she and Chum patrolled the beach, looking for nests. "The tides are right and so are the currents and water temperature. And according to my notes, by this time last year, Nate and I had found eleven nests with a total of ninety-six eggs."

She flipped back through her ever-present notebook. "Not to mention, we had a full moon last month. I thought for sure when my sisters and I found that one nest yesterday, we'd find more."

She looked out over the glittering Gulf with a frown. "Where are they? Why have we only found just one nest so far?"

Chum knocked over a sand castle and smoothed the sand. "Probably because of the blue moon."

Gen stopped dead in her tracks and gaped up at the big boy. "You mean there's a second full moon this month?"

He shrugged. "Sure."

She tapped her pencil on her notebook. "A blue moon," she muttered, "only happens once every two-point-seven years. That means it'll be a blue moon in four more nights." She frowned. "How could I have missed that? Could that have thrown off the turtles?"

"Don't feel bad, Genesis," he said. "You can't know everything. My daddy says when there is a blue moon, it makes the fish act strange, so why not turtles?"

The two walked along the shore, watching for turtle tracks. Gen's mind was still mulling over the unlikely proposition that she didn't know everything — especially when it came to turtles and astronomical phenomena — when Chum squatted down and studied something in the sand.

"Why do you reckon the tracks are going the wrong way?"

She studied the turtle tracks that were not heading inland as they should be, but were headed out to sea. "Maybe she already laid her eggs." She walked away from the shoreline in search of a nest. None was found. Anywhere.

Every set of tracks the two came across in the wet sand told the same tale: The turtle had come ashore and then, for some unknown reason, had done a U-turn and headed back out to the Gulf without laying a single solitary egg or digging a nest.

"Did you notice if all the tracks were like that, Charles?"

Chum shook his head. "I'll go look."

He trotted back along the beach, turned around, and trotted back to Gen. "Yep, they're all like that."

"And no nests?"

He shook his head.

She looked up and down the beach and then out to the heaving swells. "Something's not right," she said, plucking at an eyebrow.

"Like something's spooked them," he agreed. "But what?"

Once again, Gen pulled out her note pad and flipped back through the pages until she came to the page from the night before, up on the roof of the church.

She chewed the end of her pencil. "I noted last night at my weather station that the barometer was falling at point-one millibars per hour, and the swells were coming in five seconds apart."

"So?" Chum asked, even though he had absolutely no idea what she was talking about.

"*So,*" she said, "tonight, before I came down here, I checked the barometer again. Now it's falling by point-two millibars per hour. And I clocked wind gusts at thirty-four miles per hour."

"What does all that mean?"

Gen rubbed the sand from her glasses. "If I didn't know better, I'd say it means there's a hurricane coming."

Chum laughed. "Hurricanes don't come in the spring. Everybody knows that. Hurricane season is months and months away."

"Well *duh*," she snapped. "I know that, but the facts are the facts."

"I may not be as book smart as *you* are, Genesis Beam, and I may not have a fancy-schmancy weather station on top of my house, but I know the weather. And hurricanes *don't* come in the spring!"

Gen slapped her notebook shut. She stood and staggered in the wind. "It's not," she yelled above a particularly robust gust of wind, "beyond the realm of possibility for a —"

"Yes it is," he snapped.

"I beg to differ," Gen said, fists balled up, just itching for a fight. She couldn't believe she'd overlooked something as phenomenal as a blue moon. It was all because of this business with Nate and the lightning strike and luck (good and bad) and the pain of his words and not being best friends anymore and —

The wind snatched her ever-present notebook from her hand and sent it skipping across the sand.

"Holy Einstein!" she cried.

Chum sprinted after the errant notebook and snatched it up just before a wave claimed it as its own. He brushed off the wet sand and seaweed and held it out to Gen.

The smartest girl in Franklin County looked at the boy standing in front of her — wet, wind-rumpled, sand-coated, a sorry sight indeed — and all the fight went out of her.

"Thanks, Charles," she said, taking the notebook from his hand. And then she did something she rarely ever did. One might even say a once-in-a-blue-moon kind of rarely. She took his hand. "Come on, let's go back to the church. I bet Mama's baked something wonderful."

CHAPTER 21

Nate listened to the wind howl and race around the trailer. He slid another piece of bread into the toaster, pushed down the lever, and waited.

Ding! Out shot the toast. It landed fair and square in the center of his paper plate. The toast fairly wiggled as it reveled in its golden perfection. Just like the other twelve pieces piled on the table.

He sighed. "No offense," he said, "but being perfect is nothing special anymore."

Still, he could just hear Gen's voice saying, *It's just coincidence, Nathaniel, that they're all perfect. The odds are in your favor that one piece will end up burnt.* Like before.

He slid the last piece of bread from the bag into the toaster. He pushed down the lever.

The front door flew open.

Ding! sang the toaster.

"Whoowee!" Grandpa said, pushing the door closed. "I haven't seen wind like that in a long time." He took off his raincoat and hung it on the peg by the door. He looked like a wild man. "I don't know what's blowing in, but it's a doozy."

Nate offered the old fisherman a piece of toast.

Grandpa eyed the tower of perfect toast, then took the slice. "Thank you, Nate. And put a pot of water on the stove for coffee, would you? I'm chilled through. That ornery new truck refused to start this evening."

"What's wrong with it?" Nate asked from the kitchen.

"I'll be dipped if I know. Everything checked out fine. No missing parts. It's like it just decided it didn't want to go anywhere."

Nate could hear Gen say, *A truck can't decide anything because a truck doesn't have a brain.* Oh, how he missed the comfort of her certainty now that nothing made a bit of sense.

"Alfred never pulled a stunt like that," Grandpa grumbled. He pulled off his black rubber boots streaked with dried salt water and rubbed his foot. "The way my arthritis is acting up, I'd think a hurricane was coming in."

Nate handed his grandfather a cup of steaming hot coffee. "That's crazy. Hurricane season isn't until later in the summer," he pointed out, none too kindly. "It's just May."

Grandpa rubbed his foot and grimaced. "Just saying, is all. No need to get snappish." It had not escaped the old man's notice that lately his grandson was moody and short-tempered — two things the boy had never been before the lightning.

Friday night, as soon as her parents and all of the children were asleep, Gen climbed out her bedroom window and up onto the roof of the church. She crept over to her homemade weather station, switched on her head lamp, and peered at the barometer. "Holy Einstein," she whispered. "It's falling by half a millibar per hour." She checked the wind speed on the anemometer. *Steady winds at thirty-three mph from the Gulf,* she noted on her notebook. She switched off her head lamp and stared up at the sky. "What's coming?" she asked the moon and stars. It couldn't really be a hurricane, could it? Not this time of year. Plus, that weatherman on the Panama City station hadn't said anything about it on the news.

"Granted, he's not the most accurate meteorologist in the world," Gen muttered. "But even *he* couldn't miss a hurricane, could he?"

CHAPTER 22

The next morning, Nate did not hear the mockingbird singing in the magnolia tree. He did not hear Grandpa banging his crab traps and fishing gear into the truck. He did not hear Miss Trundle calling her cats, or the Nguyen kids playing. It was far, far too quiet for a Saturday morning at the Sweet Magnolia RV and Trailer Park.

He pushed his sheets back and looked out the window. The clouds lay low, heavy, and wet; the wind blew steady and hard.

He stuck his lucky rabbit's foot in his pocket, said good morning to his parents' photo, and pulled on his clothes. His head hurt like the dickens. The scars on his hand buzzed like bees.

His grandpa had left a note on the kitchen table — *Down at the docks.* Nate forced down a glass of chocolate milk and headed out. The wind about snatched him up when he stepped out the door. He held tight to his bicycle to keep from blowing away.

The wind pushed Nate and his bike out of the Sweet Magnolia RV and Trailer Park and down the road. It pulled and pushed him this way and that until he skidded to a halt at the docks. He spotted his grandfather bent over the open hood of the shiny red truck, cussing up a storm.

"You ornery bucket of bolts. You good-for-nothing, fancy-pantsy, high-fangled piece of plastic! I swear to Detroit, I'll sell you for scrap — don't think I won't."

"Grandpa," Nate said, pulling on the old man's sleeve.

His grandpa jerked his head up in surprise, roundly smacking it on the hood of the chastised truck. "Blue blazes, boy, don't sneak up on me like that!"

"Grandpa," he said into the wind, "get behind the wheel. Start it up when I tell you to."

The old man rubbed the top of his head and studied the pale boy. "Nate, you don't really believe in all that Midas touch malarkey, do you?"

He shrugged. "Just try, Grandpa."

Nate laid his hand on the truck's engine. "Grandpa was

right about you. You think you're better than us." He jig-gled a wire here, shook a connection there. The ornery truck gave a little hiccup.

"Crank her up, Grandpa," he hollered over the wind.

Despite the truck's best efforts to do otherwise, the engine turned over. Grandpa left the truck running and came over to Nate. He gave his shoulder a little pat. "Well, I reckon if nothing else, you have a promising future in auto mechanics."

"Yes sir," Nate agreed. "You going out fishing, Grandpa?" he asked as they packed the tools away in the truck.

Grandpa shook his head. "No sir, not today. Things don't feel right." His dark eyes took in the angry Gulf, the sodden sky, and the squadron of pelicans passing overhead. "All the birds are heading inland," he said. "Strange . . ." He pulled his grandson close. "Let's head over to the Laughing Gull and see what their TV says."

As Nate and his grandpa headed across the parking lot, a voice hallooed above the wind: "Jonah! Wait up!" Rem Bailey, Chum, and several other boat captains strode toward them.

"Jonah," Rem Bailey asked, "what do you make of this weather? Have you ever seen the like?" The wind snatched

Mr. Bailey's hat right off his head and sent it swirling toward the docks.

Grandpa pulled on his ponytail, something he was inclined to do when worried and baffled. "It's strange, all right," he agreed. "And not just the weather. The birds are all heading toward Apalachicola like their tail feathers are on fire."

"Same with the dolphins," Big Jim Sands hollered over the wind. "I saw them all heading over to the bay like they were being chased by killer whales."

Chum Bailey's daddy held up his crab-claw hand and said, "Only time my hand hurts this much is when a hurricane's coming. It's a better predictor than those weathermen on TV."

The men looked at each other nervously. Finally, Rem Bailey said what they all were thinking but didn't want to say. "If I didn't know better, I'd swear there's a hurricane coming."

"Y'all reckon we should move our boats inland?" Grandpa asked.

"Better safe than sorry," Big Jim Sands said.

Sunday morning, as most of the good citizens of Paradise Beach attended church or synagogue, the wind howled.

Mothers in their pews held their children just a little closer as the windows rattled; men glanced nervously at the rain-streaked stained-glass windows. By evening, the winds shrieked and the moon and stars were hidden behind heavy, ominous clouds.

Nate and Grandpa were busy stowing the bait buckets and crab traps underneath their trailer during a lull in the rain. Suddenly, the emergency siren at the firehouse shrieked.

"What you think that's all about?" Nate asked.

"One way to find out," his grandpa answered. "Throw your bike in the back of the truck and let's go see what's what."

"Great granny's garters," Grandpa said as they parked on Main Street. It looked like the wind had scoured out every resident of Paradise Beach from the town's nooks and crannies and blown them toward the town hall. Councilman Lamprey held tight to his wife for ballast, Miss Lillian clutched the mayor's collar, Pastor Jimmy and Rabbi Levine linked arms and bowed their heads into the wind and rain. Mr. Woods staggered out of the hardware store, Monk and Toots tucked tight under his arms. Folks poured out of the Laughing Gull Grill, the post office, the Sand Flea Hotel, and

June's Back Porch and were fairly pushed to the town hall by the wind. Before long just about every person in town dripped and huddled nervously in the meeting room.

Almost everybody.

Gen stood wet and shivering in front of her parents. Her notebook shook in her hands. "The barometer is fa-fa-falling now at one-point-five mi-mi-mi-millibars per hour," she reported through her chattering teeth.

Her mother fussed and fumed over her with a towel. "Lord have mercy, Gen, sometimes I think you don't have the sense God gave a goose!"

"Sure doesn't," Ruth agreed.

"Yes she does," Rebecca said.

Gen turned to her father. "Daddy, there's a hurricane co-coming."

The reverend gently removed the glasses from her wet face and frowned. "You have no business being out on that rooftop in a storm like this, young lady."

"But Daddy —"

"I told you a long time ago to take that weather station

down," Mrs. Beam said to her husband, sharp as a snapping turtle.

"She did," Levi and Joshua said.

Wind shook the entire building. Mrs. Beam clutched the twin boys to her. "Lord have mercy," she whispered.

The phone rang. Reverend Beam picked up. "Reverend Beam speaking." All six pairs of eyes fixed on his face.

"Is that right?" he said with a frown. "Well, that doesn't seem very likely." He studied his dripping daughter. "But yes, we'll get over there right away." He hung up the phone and rubbed at the frown on his face. "Everyone's gathering over at the town hall. Seems they're worried about the weather, and the basement there is the safest place to be." He and his wife exchanged a worried look.

"Boys," Mrs. Beam commanded, "y'all get changed out of those filthy clothes and put something decent on. Girls, wash your hands and get something to occupy yourselves. We may be over there awhile." And for once, the twins (both sets) did exactly as they were told without one argument.

Mrs. Beam surveyed Gen with a sigh. "What am I going to do about you?"

Councilman Lamprey banged his hand on the wooden desk in the town hall meeting room. "Folks," he called, "I need everyone to take their seats so we can discuss this in an orderly fashion."

No one listened. Everyone was arguing over whether or not there could be or ever had been a hurricane in the spring.

Nate put his hands over his ears. His head pounded and his stomach turned. His lightning scars burned and buzzed like blazes.

Chum sat down next to him and touched his shoulder. "You okay?"

He shook his head, then regretted it. "There's a storm coming," he whispered. "A huge one. I can feel it."

Chum nodded. "Yeah, my daddy says all the signs are there for a hurricane, but it can't be a hurricane 'cause it's spring."

"I know that, but . . ." Nate licked his lips.

"Daddy says the last time a hurricane hit in the spring was over a hundred years ago. It only happens once in . . ." Chum stopped. Gen's words came back to him: *It'll be a blue moon in four nights.* This night. ". . . a blue moon," he finished.

And then he remembered the argument he'd had with Gen, the smartest person he'd ever known, out there on the dunes, with all her talk about millibars and barometric pressure and such. Chum gripped Nate's trembling shoulder. "Gen said a hurricane's coming too. All those instruments in her weather station said so."

"Then it must be," Nate said.

The wind shrieked and howled. A window blew out on the second floor. The mayor, in his infinite wisdom, tucked his tail between his legs and crawled under the table, shaking.

"What kind of mayor does that?" Mr. Sands said, pointing accusingly at the dog.

Nate couldn't bear seeing the dog quivering with fright just like he did. "Spunk up," he whispered to himself. He pushed out of his chair and said as loud as he could, "He's scared because there's a hurricane coming!"

"That can't be," Mrs. Belk said, looking from the mayor to Nate. "It's spring."

"Yes ma'am, I know, but —"

"Ridiculous!" Mr. Sands declared. "Any fool knows hurricanes only come in the late summer and fall."

Grandpa jumped to his feet. "You calling my boy a fool, Sands?" His eyes spit daggers.

Chum Bailey jumped to his feet too. "It's true," he said. "There *is* a hurricane coming. Genesis Beam said so, and she's the smartest person I know."

Gen.

Nate looked around the packed hall of confused faces. He did not see his friend's face among them. Just like the barometric pressure, his stomach plummeted.

"The dolphins were heading over to the bay side like they were being chased by a killer whale," Rem Bailey pointed out.

"And the birds have been heading inland," Big Jim Sands said.

"Aw, for Pete's sake, Daddy," Mr. Sands said. "There wasn't a word about it on the TV, and you can bet that if a hurricane was coming in the spring —"

The double doors to the meeting room flew open. Mr. Billy stood wide-eyed in the doorway holding his portable radio aloft. "There's a hurricane coming, and it's heading straight for Paradise Beach!"

Everyone crowded around Mr. Billy. A voice crackled over

the radio: "... and this once-in-a-century hurricane — yes, folks, y'all heard me right, I said *hurricane* — is heading straight for the little town of Paradise Beach. With uncanny accuracy and speed, I might add."

"Lord help us," Pastor Jimmy whispered.

"Saints preserve us," Father Donovan said, looking up at the ceiling.

"The Lord helps those who help themselves," the good Reverend Beam intoned, heading toward the basement doors.

"It's those astronauts flying around up there, I tell you," old man Marler reminded the crowd. And for once, they wondered if he just might be right.

"It's going to take a miracle for Paradise Beach to survive a direct hit," the voice on the radio declared.

The mayor whimpered from under the table.

"Did you hear that?" Mrs. Belk cried. "He said only a miracle will save us now."

Everyone turned to the miracle boy, the boy who had been struck by a bolt of lightning on his eleventh birthday on a clear and cloudless day. And had survived.

But Nate was gone.

CHAPTER 23

While the adults had squabbled and squawked, fussed and fought, Nate had made his way over to the Beam twins, playing jacks in the corner.

"Ruthie," he said, "where's Gen?"

Ruth tossed the ball and scooped up a handful of jacks. "She's worried about that turtle nest we found the other day. She went out looking for you."

"That's right," Rebecca agreed. "It's the only one found so far, and *I* discovered it."

Ruth nodded. "She didn't see you when we got here, so she snuck out when Mama and Daddy were talking to Rabbi Levine. She made us promise not to tell."

For a split second, Nate froze, then dashed out the front doors, into the maelstrom. Except for blowing plastic bags and other garbage, nothing stirred on the street.

He grabbed his bike out of the back of the truck and threw his leg over his bicycle seat. "Oh, Gen, why the heck are you out looking for me?" As if she were right there beside him, he heard her simply say, *Because weirdos and losers stick together through thick and through thin.*

Just as he was about to push off, he heard a voice behind him say, "Where the heck are you going, Sparky?"

Ricky Sands.

"I gotta go find Gen," he said.

"You're crazier than she is if you're going out in this storm," Ricky said. "Didn't you hear in there? A hurricane is bearing down on us."

Nate squinted at the boy through the blowing wind and rain. Oh, but his head hurt so very badly, and his stomach felt like it was full of lively fish, and every flash of lightning turned his bones to jelly. It would be so easy to get off the bicycle and go back into the safety of the building and the comfort of his grandpa.

He looked at the building and at the boy standing there, now soaked to the bone, holding out a hand in something like friendship.

He squared his shoulders and set his feet upon the pedals. "I can't, Ricky," he said. "Gen needs those turtles, and I need Gen."

Now he pedaled out into the wild heart of the storm. The wind blew so hard and the rain lashed so mightily, Nate couldn't tell where he began and the storm ended. Palm trees were bent nearly doubled over. Mr. Billy's plastic chair blew across the street and busted out the window of Jean's Drugstore. A power line snapped and sparked.

"Please," he pleaded to whatever powers were afoot that night, "just let me find Gen."

Genesis Beam pushed with all her might against the wind, sometimes stopping to cling to a tree during a particularly strong gust. Finally, through sheets of rain, she saw the sign for the Sweet Magnolia RV and Trailer Park. Except the wind had blown out most of the letters. Now it read ET MAG V ARK. "Holy Einstein," she said.

She made her way to Nate and his grandpa's trailer. She figured the chances of them still being there were about a million to one (more or less), but she hadn't seen them at the town hall, and Nate was the only one who understood about the turtles.

Tossing a prayer heavenward, she said, "Please let them be there." But as soon as she saw the door to their trailer standing wide open to the storm, she knew this prayer had not been answered.

"Dang it." Poor Gen stood utterly exhausted and soaked to the bone. Moon-white petals from the sweet magnolia tree flew and swirled around her like angel wings.

Suddenly, the wind stopped and the clouds parted. She looked up to see the moon peering down upon her. Gen knew in her Gen mind that the eye of the storm was passing over, that it was purely a meteorological phenomenon. But just for that minute, she looked up into the face of the moon — a blue moon at that — and allowed herself to be captured in wonderment.

A wind chime tinkled. She blinked. "The turtles!" She spied a large bait bucket underneath the trailer and grabbed it. She dashed from the empty trailer park to the beach. If she could just get to the nest of eggs before the eye passed and the winds came back, she might be able to save them.

Nate raced to the trailer park along the crushed oyster shell road until he skidded to a stop in front of his trailer. The door stood open. Chairs had blown off the porch. He raced into the trailer, calling for his friend, hoping she'd taken refuge there.

He checked all four of the trailer's rooms, including his own room. No Gen. "Dang and double dang," he cursed as the wind began to moan. Thunder rumbled and lightning flashed.

He rubbed his throbbing head and willed his churning, roiling stomach to behave. He double-checked that he had the rabbit's foot in his pocket and slipped the framed photograph of his parents inside his shirt. With one last look at his room — a room he suddenly realized he loved — he raced back out into the storm.

"I've got to get to the eggs!" Gen cried into the newly energized wind. A bolt of lightning flashed directly overhead. A gust of wind pushed her down onto the wet sand.

Genesis Beam, not only the smartest girl in Franklin County, but also the most stubborn too, crouched on hands and knees, sobbing. "I can't. I just can't do this by myself."

A bolt of lightning streaked past and struck the mast of a beached sailboat twenty feet away at the foot of her and Nate's sand dune. Gen's hair stood on end. Her feet tingled.

She shook with fright and squeezed her eyes shut. *How did he survive being struck — even indirectly — by such a force?* she wondered.

"But he did," she shouted to the wind. She pulled herself to her feet, grabbed the bucket, and set off for the nest of eggs.

Nate stood atop the tallest dune in Paradise Beach scouring the shoreline for his friend. Twice the wind blew him to the sand, but he pulled himself back up. *Spunk up, Sparky,* he said to himself. *Spunk up.*

But then the lightning came, all around. It flashed to the side of him, to the back of him, and then right out front, as if taking the measure of the boy. Like a hound dog looking for its long-lost master.

"Oh good Lord," he moaned, and dropped to his knees. "I can't," he said, burying his face in his hands. "I can't do this."

The storm had returned with a vengeance. Froth-capped waves reared and pounded the beach with a violence he had rarely witnessed. Thunder roared overhead with lightning right on its heels. The wind shrieked.

"Nate! Nate!"

Or was it the wind? He looked in the direction of the voice. A particularly showy flash of lightning lit the beach like daylight.

And there, right there, Nate saw Gen clinging to the beached sailboat. Waves moved in higher and higher toward her.

"Oh good gravy," he whimpered. "She can't swim. Gen!" Nate cried. "Hold on, I'm coming!" He flew down the sand dune to the girl. A gust of wind pushed so hard at his back, he would later swear his feet didn't touch the ground at all.

Nate squinted through the stinging rain at Gen, clutching a bucket full of wet sand and white turtle eggs with one hand and the mast of the boat with the other, water swirling around her legs. "We've got to get out of here," he said. "We've got to get away from that metal mast."

Lightning streaked and splintered overhead.

"I know that," she said. "Metal is a natural conductor of electricity." She held the bucket out to her friend. "But look," she said, rain slashing her face. "I saved the eggs."

Nate took the bucket and grabbed her hand tight in his. "You're the best friend a turtle could ever have," he said. He tightened his grip on Gen's hand. "Let's get out of here!"

Then came a loud *pop* and bright flash of light, and a deafening clap of thunder shook the earth. Nate felt an all-too-familiar hand grab him (none too gently, again) by the arm, twirl him up, and fling him away from Gen.

CHAPTER 24

The last things Genesis Magnolia Beam remembered were the feel of Nate's hand gripping hers and the brightest flash of light she'd ever seen engulfing them.

Then she felt herself rising, rising above the wet sand, as if someone were pulling her up and up with a thousand strings fine as spider's silk. The strings pulled her free of her chest, free of her stomach, arms, legs, and finally free of her skin, with a soap-bubble *pop!*

Suddenly, a hundred million tiny lights danced around her. She remembered Nate saying, "It was like every lightning bug in the United States was around me," after he'd come home from the hospital.

He was exactly right, she thought. She started to feel ashamed of how she'd ridiculed Nate when he told her that. But then the lights tickled her arms and back and legs like her cats at home, all rubbing up against her at once. It filled her with a peace and joy she'd never before felt.

For once, Gen's mind did not want to find the logical explanation for what she was experiencing. She did not care if it was the result of neurological misfiring in her brain, or if it was truly the result of magic. She just wanted it to go on forever and ever, and sing hallelujah.

CHAPTER 25

The first thing Nate was aware of was something warm and thick stroking his cheek over and over and over. The second thing he was aware of was a smell like rotten fish and seaweed pushing against his face on hot breath.

He opened his eyes. The mayor of Paradise Beach licked his face and wagged his whole body with joy.

He threw his arms around the dog's neck and pulled himself upright. To his astonishment, the wind had stopped. Rain no longer lashed the beach, the Gulf was calm as a cat, and the full blue moon shone bright. "Jiminy Christmas," he whispered. "The hurricane's gone." He looked into the grizzled face of the old dog. "How could that be?"

Before the mayor could answer, Nate heard someone cry, "Nate! Gen! Where the heck are you?"

Gen.

Nate staggered to his feet. Every inch of his body was on fire, especially his chest. He looked down at his empty hand. "Gen?"

The bluish light of the once-in-a-blue-moon moon revealed a sickening sight: Gen, the smartest girl in Franklin County and maybe even in all of Florida, Gen, his best and steadfast friend, lay crumpled on the sand, smoke rising from her wet clothes.

"Gen!" he cried. He pulled his legs beneath him and ran, stumbled, and lurched to the broken body of his friend. He turned her over. "Gen," he sobbed.

Her eyes — eyes that were now unaccountably silver — stared with a mixture of astonishment and fear and joy into the Great Mysterious.

Nate knew exactly where she was, for hadn't he himself been there just weeks before? He gathered his friend, his very best friend on God's green earth, into his arms and shook her. "Come back, Gen," he sobbed. "Please come back. You brought *me* back, remember?"

He laid her out flat on the wet sand. Just like she had done for him, he tipped her head back and pinched her nose closed. Then he blew in her mouth once, twice, three times. He pushed on her chest over and over. *Breathe, breathe, breathe. Pump, pump, pump.* "Come on, Gen," he pleaded. *Breathe, breathe, breathe. Pump, pump, pump.*

Nate heard a wailing in the distance. Was he crying for Gen or were his ears ringing? And then he saw flashing red lights.

"Please, Gen," he said with a tear-filled voice. "Come back."

Chum Bailey flopped down next to him in the wet sand. "Lord Almighty, Nate," he said. "The whole town's been looking for you!"

"Gen," Nate whimpered.

Chum's gaze fell on Gen, sprawled like a wet rag doll in the sand. "Oh good Lord," he whispered.

Then Chum Bailey, the biggest boy in fifth grade, scooped Gen up as if she weighed nothing and took off at a dead run for the ambulance.

The mayor woofed.

Nate tried to stand but his knees wouldn't hold him. He fell back onto the sand, his head cradled softly as if by a pair of warm hands.

He dragged his heavy eyes open and looked up into the most wonderful face he had ever seen. A face bright with the luminescence that rode the waves at night; a smile as eternal as a dolphin's smile; eyes as old and wise as a loggerhead turtle's.

He tried to reach his hand up to the face. "Grandpa?"

A hand warm and strong came to rest on his cheek. "Hush now, Nathaniel, everything's going to be fine . . . just fine."

"But Gen," he said as the energy drained from his body. "What about Gen?"

Nate thought he heard his grandpa say something from very far away. He heard the mayor bark: "Roof! Roof! A-roooo!"

"Gen," he whispered.

As the last twinkling light in his body faded, Nate heard the sound of a hundred turtle flippers rowing toward Paradise Beach.

CHAPTER 26

Nate woke to the sound of a mockingbird singing hallelujah in the magnolia tree. He heard Miss Trundle calling, "Here, Fluffy, here, kitty, kitty, kitty. Mama's got something good for you to eat." He heard little Jimmy Nguyen call with excitement, "Look what I found!" And he heard the growl and whine of a chain saw not far away.

He propped himself up on one elbow and looked around his tiny bedroom — *his bedroom*, not a hospital room. He looked at his hands. No bandages. He wiggled his toes. Everything worked just fine.

And then he heard his grandpa cussing up a storm in the kitchen. "You worthless old thing. Why can't you make just one piece of toast without burning it?"

Nate sat bolt upright. He could hear! Even though he'd been struck by lightning again, he could hear!

He could hear the mockingbird and Miss Trundle and Jimmy Nguyen and every word his grandpa said.

"Grandpa!" he hollered.

Grandpa threw the door open and rushed to Nate's bed. He took the boy's hand and said, "Welcome back, son." His grandpa grinned a grin wide and bright as the Gulf of Mexico. "I was beginning to think you were going to sleep until Christmas." He smoothed Nate's hair away from his forehead.

He looked from his grandpa's face to the window of his bedroom. "But how did I get here?"

"Don't you remember?"

He shook his head, and instantly regretted it.

"Chum Bailey found y'all down on the beach. He told me where you were, and I carried you up to the ambulance. Pretty much everybody in town was down at the beach by then, including Dr. Silverstein. He checked you over real good. Seems the metal frame of that photograph you had under your shirt somehow protected you from the lightning. Talk about lucky. You didn't need to go to the hospital, so they just took Gen."

Gen. Nate's heart stuttered. "What about her?" he croaked. He remembered her lifeless body and her silvered eyes staring with longing and wonder.

Grandpa shook his head and wiped at his eyes.

Nate felt his entire world fall away. "Is she . . . is she dead, Grandpa?" Tears spilled down his cheeks.

Grandpa clasped Nate's hand in his. "No, son, she's not dead. The doctors say the CPR you gave her most likely saved her life."

The world realigned itself. Nate let out a sigh of relief.

"But she wasn't as lucky as you. She took a direct hit from that lightning bolt," Grandpa said, not looking at the hopeful eyes of the boy.

"Yeah, but she's going to be okay, isn't she?" After all, except for some burns and briefly losing his hearing and all, he'd been fine. Sort of.

Grandpa swallowed, hard. "She's in a coma, Nate." He wiped at his eyes again. "When they first got her over to the hospital, the doctors put her in a coma to help her brain heal. But now they're trying to bring her around, and she won't wake up."

Nate pushed the covers aside and did his level best to leap out of bed. His legs buckled beneath him. Grandpa swept him back into bed.

"I got to get to the hospital, Grandpa," he pleaded. "Maybe my touch can heal her like it did with the *Bay Leaf* and your truck and the toaster, and . . ." His voice trailed off as Grandpa pushed him back against the pillows.

"What you *got* to do is *rest*," Grandpa said as he fussed with the blankets. "Besides, the hurricane carried that truck off somewhere — and good riddance too, if you ask me — and the toaster is burning up the toast again."

Nate had a million more questions to ask, but first he had to convince Grandpa to take him over to the hospital in Panama City.

If only he could keep his eyes open . . .

When next Nate awoke, it was to the most wonderful smell. It was not the smell of burnt toast or fried baloney. He swung his legs over the bed and gingerly stood. His whole body ached, but this time, his legs held firm.

Carefully, he followed his nose down the hallway. Miss Trundle bustled around the tiny kitchen, creating culinary wonders.

Nate's stomach rumbled.

Miss Trundle spun around. "Oh! You're awake!" she said with delight. Then she frowned and clapped her hands. "You get yourself on that couch, young man. You shouldn't be up."

Nate curled up on the couch and watched her slide a skillet of buttermilk corn bread from the oven. "Mmm . . ." Nate said, drinking in the smell. "That's what smells so good."

She smiled. She took two plates from the cupboard. "And we've got a pot of my prize-winning seafood gumbo too." She ladled soup into bowls and buttered the corn bread.

Nate snapped the TV trays together. His mouth watered from the wonder of Miss Trundle's gumbo and corn bread in his house.

They ate in silence. Finally, after his belly felt like it was about to pop, Nate pushed his bowl aside. "Miss Trundle," he said, "I got to get over to the hospital to see Gen."

She sighed. "That poor, poor child." She shook her head, her curls bouncing. "The doctors don't know why she won't wake up. Her heart and everything seem fine, as far as they can tell. They said that, because of lack of oxygen, her brain might be a bit scatter-wonky, but" — she leaned in to Nate confidentially — "just between you and me, I've always thought that child was a bit, well, *strange*."

"But I've got to see her," he said.

Miss Trundle gathered up the plates. "You're in no shape to go over there, Nate. Besides, your grandfather's there right now, probably praying with Reverend Beam. Not much else anybody can do." She covered the skillet of corn bread with foil. "They say it could take a miracle for her to come out of that coma unscathed. But you never know. . . . I mean, look at that hurricane."

"What do you mean?" Nate asked.

She turned to him. "Well, it was the strangest thing: It hit Paradise Beach head-on, just like they'd predicted. But then it just *left*. Hardly did any damage at all. Few trees down here and there, and your grandpa's new truck is Lord knows where — probably Sopchoppy." She shook her head in wonderment. "But not a single soul hurt. Except Gen."

The next morning, Nate felt a bit stronger. His body no longer felt hot all over, just kind of tingly. "I've got to get to Gen," he said to the mockingbird and the magnolia tree and the singed photograph of his parents.

His grandpa was just finishing off his third cup of coffee and a plate of Miss Trundle's buttermilk corn bread.

"Morning, boy. How you feeling?" he asked with worried eyes.

"Good," Nate said. "Better."

Grandpa plopped the blue sombrero on his head. "That's good. I got to head down to the docks to help Big Jim with some repairs. His boat slip took the biggest hit. The rest of us were pretty darned lucky. We're all pitching in to give him a hand." He rubbed his hand over his stubbly face. "Funny how a hurricane can bring out the best in folks."

"Grandpa, how's Gen? Did she wake up yet?"

Grandpa sighed. "Not yet."

"Dang," Nate said. "That's not good, is it?"

His grandpa shook his head, his eyes full of sorrow. "No, son, it isn't. The doctors say every hour she stays in that coma, she's less likely to come out of it."

Nate grasped the old man's arm. "Grandpa, I just got to get over to the hospital to see her. Can't you take me?"

Grandpa smoothed the boy's troubled hair away from his face. "I have to go down to the docks to help. We'll go over there first thing tomorrow morning, okay?" Before Nate could answer, his grandpa gave him a pat on the shoulder and headed out.

It surely was not okay. "I got to get to Gen *now*, not tomorrow," Nate said to the toaster. "But how?"

A half hour later, the answer knocked on the trailer door. It came in the form of a large boy with a smile as warm and sweet as a puppy.

"Hey, Nate," Chum Bailey said. In his arms he held the seagoing cat, Mr. Bowditch. "We thought you might like some company."

"Yeah, Sparky."

Nate looked from Chum to the cat and blinked.

Chum stepped into the trailer. Ricky Sands followed in his wake.

Nate's mouth dropped open. Ricky Sands in *his* trailer, looking like he dropped by all the time, which he surely did not.

Ricky smiled a crooked smile. "Better shut your mouth, Sparky, or a fly'll get in."

"But what are you doing here?" Nate asked. "Why aren't you in school?"

"They cancelled school this week," Ricky said. "I had to come see for myself what a person who's been struck by lightning twice looks like."

"I wonder what the odds of that are? We should ask Gen," Chum said.

Nate said all in a rush, "Yeah, but she's all the way over at the hospital in Panama City and she's in a coma and she won't wake up and the doctors say if she doesn't wake up soon she probably never will and I don't have any way of getting over there and I *have* to try to wake her up." He slumped down onto the couch like a deflated balloon.

Ricky held up a shiny silver key and smiled. "Then let's go."

CHAPTER 27

Nate sat in between Ricky Sands and Chum Bailey on the fine leather seats of a slightly used pickup truck, Mr. Bowditch purring in his lap.

"Um, you got a driver's license, Ricky?" he asked as they crossed the bridge to Apalachicola.

Ricky shrugged. "Nah, I'm too young to have a driver's license. I know how to drive, though. My grandpa taught me how to drive his boat when I was nine, and I've been driving cars around my dad's dealership for almost that long." He leaned forward and peered through the windshield. "Course, I've never driven this far before."

Chum rubbed Mr. Bowditch on the top of his head, just where he liked it. "When my mama finds out about me being in on this, she'll most likely skin me alive."

"I don't want you to get skinned alive — either of you," Nate said.

"I don't care," Chum said. "You and Gen are my best friends." Still, he ducked down out of sight as they drove past the Piggly Wiggly where his mother worked.

"Chum, how did you know I was out looking for Gen that night?" Nate asked.

"Ricky," he said, sitting back up. "He came and got me after he talked to you outside. Then I noticed Gen wasn't there."

Nate nodded. "But how did you know to find us at the beach?"

"The mayor," Chum simply said.

Nate watched the signs for Port Saint Joe, Beacon Hill, and Mexico Beach come and go. He had no idea what they'd do once they got to the hospital. How would he know what room she was in? And would her parents let him see her? Oh, they could be in for a whole boatload of trouble, he knew. He broke out into a cold sweat.

An hour after leaving Paradise Beach, Ricky whipped the truck into a parking space at the Panama City Hospital.

He grinned at Nate and Chum. "We made it!" High fives all around.

"You go on in. We'll be right behind you."

It was then Nate noticed Ricky's knuckles were white as the sand. He touched Ricky's arm. "You did real good, Ricky. Your daddy would be proud of how well you drove."

The bright fluorescent lights and antiseptic smell of the hospital brought back a storm of memories — not good memories — to Nate. His lightning scars burned. His head throbbed. Right at that very moment, he wanted nothing more than to walk back outside and go home. But Gen was somewhere here in this place, and he meant to find her.

Nate gathered up twice-struck courage, squared his hunched shoulders, and walked up to the nurses' station. A woman with little glasses perched on the end of her long nose looked up as he cleared his throat. "I'm here to see a patient," Nate said with all the authority he could muster.

The nurse surveyed him through narrowed eyes. "You are, huh? And who might that patient be?"

"Gen. I mean, Genesis Beam. I believe she was brought in three days ago."

The woman tapped the keys on her computer. "Beam, Beam . . ." she muttered under her breath.

Nate drummed his fingers on the desk. He wondered just how many Genesis Beams there could be in the computer. Especially ones struck by lightning.

"Genesis Beam," the nurse declared, as if she had just made up the whole notion of a Genesis Beam. "Right here. The kid struck by lightning, poor thing."

"Yes ma'am," he agreed. "I'm here to see her, I just don't know what room she's in."

The nurse looked at Nate, then to the left and right of him and behind him. "Where are your parents? Minors aren't allowed to visit patients without an adult." She crossed her arms over her chest with finality.

Nate licked his lips. "Well, um, my parents are already up there visiting. I just don't know the room number." He tried to get a peek at the computer screen.

"If your parents are already up there, how did *you* get here?"

Nate gulped. This was not going well. Not well at all. "Well, you see, I —"

Just then, Chum Bailey and Ricky Sands jogged into the hospital. "Sorry we took so long, Nate," Ricky said.

The nurse narrowed her eyes to slits. "And who might *you* be?"

Ricky stood as tall as his five-foot-two inch frame would carry him, leaned in confidently to the nurse behind the desk, and said, "I'm Ricky Sands. My dad owns Crystal Sands New and Used Cars in Paradise Beach. I'm sure you've heard of it."

The nurse frowned and shot a look at Chum. "And you?"

Chum smiled. "I'm Charles Bailey, ma'am, and this here's Mr. Bowditch." At the sound of his name, the cat's head popped out of the top of the big boy's shirt.

The nurse's eyes widened. "Is that a *cat*?" she asked in a way that led the boys to believe she might be none too fond of cats.

Chum looked down at the small, furry head and paws sticking out the top of his shirt. He frowned. "Why, yes ma'am, that's just what Mr. Bowditch is." Mr. Bowditch twitched his pink little nose and whiskers.

"Young man, animals are expressly forbidden in the

hospital." She pointed her finger at the sliding glass doors. "You must take it out this instant."

Chum's frown deepened. "Ma'am, Mr. Bowditch is a *him*, not an *it*. And —"

The nurse stood, her face a fury, her fists balled on her hips. "I don't care *what* it is, take that cat —"

Clearly, the nurse had forgotten all about Nate. He peered around the computer screen. He could just make out 317.

The nurse turned back to Nate and was just about to tell him she'd had enough of all this nonsense when Mr. Bowditch decided *he'd* had quite enough of the all-too-warm confines of Chum's shirt. With one graceful leap, he pushed himself out of the boy's shirt and leapt onto the desk.

The nurse gasped. "Get that cat off my desk!" She flapped her hands at Mr. Bowditch. "Shoo! Shoo! Get away from here!"

Office doors flew open. Heads popped out of cubicles to see what all the ruckus was about.

"Go Nate!" Ricky hissed.

Under the cover of chaos, Nate dashed to the elevator and slid in. As the elevator doors closed, he heard Chum calling, "Come back, Mr. Bowditch! Come back!"

He looked at all the different buttons. On a hunch, he punched the button for the third floor and prayed, once he got there, he'd be able to find her room.

He stepped out onto the third floor. The nurse sitting behind the desk was on the phone. "There's a *what* loose downstairs?" he heard her ask.

He trotted down the hallway looking for room 317. Three-one-one, three-one-three. Three-one-four, three-one-five.

And then he saw it: room 317. He pushed the door open.

The sight that greeted him was this: The room was dark, the shades pulled. A monitor with lots of lights and bright lines and beeps lit one corner of the room. A small figure lay still as still could be beneath the crisp hospital bedsheets. And beside that figure, sitting hunched over in a chair, hunched from the weight of grief with his head in his hands, was Reverend Beam.

Nate eased the door closed and walked over to the grieving man. He touched his shoulder. "Hey," he whispered.

The reverend looked up, his eyes wide and wet.

If Nate hadn't known this was Reverend Beam, he'd never have recognized him. This face looking up at him was not the face of the man he knew. This face was not the shining beacon of hope and light and absolute certainty he counted on. This was not the face full of humor and kindness he loved almost as well as he loved the seaworn face of his grandfather. This was the face of a man utterly broken.

"Nate," the reverend said. "You're here?"

Nate tried to smile, but the muscles in his face didn't cooperate. "Yes sir, I'm here." He squeezed the man's shoulder.

The reverend blinked like he'd just woken up. He ran his hand across his face and looked around the room. "It's a nice room. Folks have been very kind," he said, nodding.

"Yes sir," Nate said. "Where's Mrs. Beam?"

The reverend looked around the room as if wondering that himself. Then he said, "Ah, she went down to the cafeteria to see if they had liverwurst on rye. She thought maybe if Gen smelled her favorite food, she'd wake up and . . ." His face crumbled.

"I'm here now, sir. Why don't you take a little break — go get some coffee or something?"

The reverend stood, a tiny light flickering in his eyes. "I'll go find Mrs. Beam. Would it be okay with you if I left for just a minute?" He reached down and touched his daughter's cheek. "I'll be right back, I promise."

The door whispered closed. The monitor beeped.

For the first time, Nate took a good look at Gen. Without her glasses, her face looked so very small and vulnerable. Spiderlike burns sprawled across her jaw. Her right arm and hand were wrapped in bandages.

But the thing that almost brought Nate to his knees was her missing eyebrows. They were completely and utterly gone. The eyebrows Mrs. Beam had worked so hard to preserve from Gen's worrying had been vaporized by the lightning.

"Oh, Gen," he said.

He sat in the chair next to his very best friend. He told her all he could remember of that night — how the lightning had struck just as he'd grabbed her hand and how the force of it had thrown him a good six feet away. How the mayor had found him there on the beach and brought him back to the world. How he'd tried his very best to do CPR on Gen just like she'd done on him.

Nate told Gen how he'd woken up in his own bed the next day, purely and totally amazed to still be alive. And how miraculous he'd thought it was — a *true* miracle — that it was the framed photograph of his long-dead parents that'd saved him.

"I figured I was the luckiest boy in the whole world," he said. "Until Grandpa told me you were in the hospital and wouldn't wake up."

He took a deep, watery breath. "I knew I had to get over here to try to fix you like I fixed the *Bay Leaf* and Grandpa's truck." He wiped at his nose. "Well, maybe I did. Or maybe it was all coincidence like you always said."

The girl lay silent as the moon.

Nate sighed. "So here I am, Gen, and I sure as heck hope that lightning didn't take my luck away." He took a deep breath, closed his eyes, and laid his hands on her good arm.

Nothing.

"Come on, Gen," he pleaded, pressing harder.

The only movement was the rising and falling of her chest.

"Dang it," Nate said in despair. He felt the burnt toast making its way up his throat. "I've run out of luck after all."

He gripped her bandaged hand in his scarred one and said into her ear, "I know exactly where you were, Genesis

Magnolia Beam, and I know how wonderful it feels. I'm sorry I brought you back, but . . ." His voice cracked and then trailed off. "Maybe you're still there and you don't want to come back, but, Gen, I need you. And the turtles need you too. You're our best friend."

One of the green ziggity lines on the monitor blipped and jumped.

"I need the smartest girl in all of Franklin County to tell me how stupid it is to believe in luck. I need you to tell me what the odds are of a hurricane coming in the spring, and what the odds are of two people getting struck by lightning at the same time."

Silence.

Nate pressed his face into his arm. "Come on, Gen. Come back. Weirdos and losers stick together through thick and through thin."

"Amen," a smoky voice said.

Nate's eyes flew open. There, gazing back at him as if from some great height, were the eyes of his best friend, Genesis Beam.

She smiled with just the tiniest corner of her mouth.

"Hey, Gen," he said with a grin that about split his face in two.

"Hey, Nathaniel," she said. The fingertips on her bandaged hand wiggled against his hand. Her fingers felt like little live coals.

The door flew open. Reverend Beam dashed in, followed by Mrs. Beam. "I'm sorry it took so long, Nate. There was some crazy fool cat loose in the cafeteria and —"

"Hey, Daddy," Gen said.

For the first time in the known history of heaven and earth, the good Reverend Beam was rendered completely speechless. Mrs. Beam dropped the plate of liverwurst on rye.

"Dear, dear God," Mrs. Beam whispered, pressing her hands to her mouth. "My baby's awake."

Nate let go of Gen's hand and stepped aside. Reverend and Mrs. Beam gathered their daughter in their arms and wept.

And for the first time in all the many years Nate had known Genesis Beam, he saw tears flow from her eyes.

Eyes unaccountably, and forever after, silver.

CHAPTER 28

Several nights later, Nate sat next to Gen's bed at the Panama City Hospital. This time the ride over from Paradise Beach had been much less exciting, with his grandpa in old Alfred.

Only he came along this time. Ricky's father had grounded him until he was thirty, and Chum's mama had, in fact, skinned him alive. Well, nearly.

"Is it true you get to go home tomorrow?" Nate asked.

"Yes," she said with a smile. "I can't wait."

He nodded, remembering how wonderful it was to get home to their little trailer and his own room, his own bed.

"Of course, there won't be any climbing on the roof to monitor my weather station, at least not for a while." She nodded toward the wheelchair waiting in the corner.

Nate flinched every time he looked at it. He really had been lucky he hadn't been hit directly by lightning like she had.

As if reading his mind, Gen said, "I only have to use it for a few weeks. It's not that big a deal." Changing the subject, she asked, "Any signs of the turtles?"

He grinned. "Lots! They're coming in like crazy now and laying eggs too."

She twisted and untwisted her blanket with her good hand. "And I'm not there to look after them. What's going to happen to them, Nathaniel?"

He smiled again and handed her the latest issue of the *Paradise Beach Herald*. The headline announced MIRACLE SAVES KIDS FROM LIGHTNING AND TOWN FROM HURRICANE!

And just below that, he pointed to a smaller headline that read TOWN HONORS LOCAL LIGHTNING GIRL BY PROTECTING TURTLES.

Gen squinted at the fuzzy newsprint. "I can't wait until I get my new glasses. Can you read it to me?"

Nate cleared his throat and read: "Everybody in Paradise Beach knows how much Genesis Beam, daughter of Reverend and Mrs. Beam, loves loggerhead turtles. She is the creator of the Turtle Rules and self-appointed guardian of the reptilian wayfarers when they visit our shores every year to lay their eggs. But no one knew just how much she loved the turtles until the recent (and unlikely) hurricane struck. To quote Charles Bailey, age twelve, 'She loves them so much, she almost got herself killed!'

"Miss Beam risked her life in the middle of Hurricane Amelia by running down to the beach and gathering up (in a bait bucket) the one nest of loggerhead turtle eggs that had been laid. During her valiant attempt to save the eggs, Miss Beam was struck by lightning.

"Because of the young girl's heroism and devotion to the turtles, the town is organizing a turtle watch in her honor. The Paradise Beach Garden and Beautification League along with Miss Ruth Beam (age six), daughter of Reverend and Mrs. Beam, are organizing the effort. 'We need folks to patrol the beaches not only to watch for turtle nests and tracks, but also to enforce Genesis's Turtle Rules,' Mrs. Belk, president of the Garden and Beautification League, declared. 'We need all hands on deck,' Big Jim Sands, captain of the *Dixie Queen*, said. 'It's what that little girl would want.'

"Hanson's Hardware is providing free flashlights and batteries for those who don't have them, and Dick McHarg, owner of the Sand Flea Motel, will provide free hot chocolate to those taking the evening watch shifts. 'I'm proud to do it,' he said. 'We're lucky as all get-out to have these turtles come back here every year.' Indeed."

"Wow," Gen whispered. "All those people are helping the turtles because of me?"

"Oh heck yeah," he said. "Ricky, Connor, and Buddy are helping out, and the whole town council."

She shook her head with the pure wonderment of it. "Maybe they aren't a band of philistines after all."

"Oh, and my teacher, Mr. Peck, is giving anyone who helps extra credit, and Miss Lillian is composing a special poem about it. There's even talk about starting an annual turtle festival."

"I guess the turtles aren't just mine and yours anymore," Gen said. "Who would have thought?"

"It's a miracle, just like my shoes," Nate said, holding his legs out straight, tapping the toes of his *two* red high-top sneakers together.

Gen shook her head. "I still can't believe you found the other shoe yesterday on the side of Highway 98." She reached up to pluck at her long-gone eyebrow. "I can't even begin to calculate those odds."

"Hey," he said, "I've been wanting to ask you. What are the odds of a person getting struck by lightning *twice*?"

Gen perked up. "Well, let's see. If the odds of a person getting struck by lightning once are about one in six hundred fifty thousand, then if you multiply that by . . ." She frowned and drew on an imaginary chalkboard in the air.

"Three hundred and sixty billion," Nate replied.

Gen's jaw dropped.

Nate blinked, then said, "Where'd that come from?"

"*You*," she said with a gasp. "How'd you know that?"

He shook his head. "I don't know. It just sort of popped into my head. But how?"

Nate waited for his friend, who was obviously chewing on this information like a dog with a particularly meaty bone, to tell him the scientific explanation for this phenomenon. Energy transference? A shifting of magnetic poles perhaps?

Gen shrugged and smiled. She looked out her hospital window into the evening sky growing as lavender as her mother's favorite going-to-church hat. "Magic, I guess."

CHAPTER 29

A week later, the residents of Paradise Beach again gathered at the Billy Bowlegs Park for a fish fry. Although the congregations of the town's three churches and one synagogue had organized the event as a fund-raiser for Reverend Beam's family, everyone agreed it was also to celebrate the town's good fortune.

Once again, table after table groaned under the bountiful weight of salads, casseroles, gumbos, mounds of biscuits, corn bread and, of course, hush puppies. The men and women of all three congregations and one synagogue had outdone themselves and glory.

Grandpa and Reverend Beam manned the vats of frying fish and hush puppies. Chum Bailey, Ricky Sands, and Jinx Malloy poured cup after cup of lemonade and iced tea.

"Hey, Sparky," Jinx said as she sloshed lemonade into a cup for Nate. "We're getting up a baseball game after everyone eats. Want to play?"

He shrugged and gripped the handles of Gen's wheelchair. "I don't think I'm lucky anymore," he said, still tasting burnt toast and sour milk from that morning.

Jinx snorted and flipped her red braids over her shoulders. "Aw heck, I never believed in all that Midas touch malarkey," she declared. She nodded at Gen. "She can play too. We can take turns pushing her around the bases. It's just for fun anyways."

"I don't think so," Nate said, moving closer to his friend and touching her arm. He knew without a doubt that 1) to go around the bases implied one would hit the ball which 2) he was pretty sure Gen would never do. "I think we'll just —"

"Heck yes!" Gen fairly yipped. Which was something he had never, ever heard Genesis Beam do. She'd also been known to giggle and guffaw and look all dreamy since the lightning strike. "We'll play. I can be a receiver or a goalie even."

Ricky groaned and Chum laughed.

The last of the sun's rays threw wide, spangled planks of light across Billy Bowlegs Park. It skipped across the gulls squabbling around the trash bins and settled lightly on the sleeping head of Brandon Sands. It touched the shoulders of Chum, Jinx, and Ricky as they picked their teams for baseball. It warmed the back of the mayor of Paradise Beach as he begged yet another hush puppy. It moved on to rest on the wide, humble shoulders of the good Reverend Beam.

Everyone grew quiet as he took the stage and stepped up to the microphone. He cleared his throat and clasped his hands in front of him. "I stand before you, friends and family, a most grateful man. A most lucky man. For we are gathered here again to celebrate not one, not two, but *three* miracles. We celebrate the town surviving a direct hit from a hurricane with barely a scratch; we celebrate the miracle of two precious children struck by lightning and living." The reverend smiled lovingly down at Nate and Gen. "For that, I will be eternally grateful."

"Amen," murmured the crowd.

Picking up steam, the reverend continued. "But truly, the greatest miracle we celebrate is the strength and compassion of our town." He spread his arms wide, taking in the entire community of Paradise Beach. "We celebrate the bounty and wonder of this place we call home and the folks we call friends and neighbors. And we count our many blessings and tender mercies, every day."

"Amen," Gen whispered. She held up her bandaged hand. "How about a high five?" she asked with a smile.

Nate grinned and pressed his scarred hand gently against hers.

A mighty crack! "Go, Gen, go!" Nate and Jinx cried.

Genesis Magnolia Beam — the smartest girl in all of Franklin County and maybe even in all of Florida — dropped the bat burning her hands. Chum and Ricky dug in shoulder to shoulder, wheeling her from base to base to base. Gen's silver eyes gleamed with a million tiny lights.

And Nathaniel Harlow, who many had said was the unluckiest boy in all of Franklin County, watched his friends with a grin wide and bright as the bay and the Gulf and all the waters beyond.

He rubbed his thumb over the knobby rabbit's foot. Yes, there were great bounties and blessings indeed. School would be out in just a few days with the whole summer stretching ahead like a brand-new world: days out on the Gulf with his grandpa and the *Sweet Jodie*, crabbing and scalloping with Chum, Ricky, and Jinx over in the bay, and at the end of the summer, the town would see the loggerhead hatchlings safely out to sea.

There would be trials too. Gen had a long summer of physical therapy ahead of her. The doctors promised if she worked hard (and when had Genesis Beam not worked hard?), her legs would be as good as new. And Nate promised her that when they were, he'd teach her to ride a bike.

And then, just then, if anyone had asked, he'd have said he sure enough was the luckiest boy in all of Franklin County, and most likely all of Florida too.

THE END

Acknowledgments

Although I feel I have been extraordinarily lucky these past few years to be able to write stories and bring them into the world, it takes a lot more than just luck! As Nate discovered, what makes you truly lucky is the miracle of friendship and community.

First, I want to thank my lovely, tenacious agent, Alyssa Eisner Henkin, who has stuck by me through thick and through thin. Amen.

I am so lucky (and yes, blessed) to once again have Arthur A. Levine as my partner in crime on this journey. Many, many thanks to "Team Levine" for making this the best possible book it could be: Nicholas Thomas, Kate Hurley, Elizabeth Starr Baer, and Ellen Duda for her inspired design.

A boatload of heartfelt thanks to my community of early readers, Jean Reagan, Lora Koehler, Chris Graham, Lisa Actor, Miss Bettis, and Molly O'Neill, for giving me invaluable feedback. I hope I've done y'all proud!

My consultant on all things fishing was my stepbrother, Captain Cliff Cox, and his boat the *Sweet Jodie*. Thanks Captain!

As always, none of this would be possible without Todd, my lucky charm.

Finally, I want to thank my mother for giving me the gift of the sea. She taught me the magic of the Gulf of Mexico, and shared her passion for its many treasures and bounties. Mama, I have no doubt your spirit lives on in every porpoise smile, in every stroke of loggerhead flippers rowing their way to the shores of the Gulf.

This book was designed by Ellen Duda. The text was set in ITC Legacy Serif LT, and the display type was set in Coop. The book was printed and bound at R. R. Donnelley in Crawfordsville, Indiana. Production was supervised by Elizabeth Starr Baer, and manufacturing was supervised by Shannon Rice.